SALVAGE JOB

A storm has left the oil tanker S.S *Craig Michael* stranded and almost blocking the only channel to the bay at Cabo Esco and the Portuguese fishing village of Porto Esco. Sent to investigate, marine insurance inspector Laird hires a diver, who meets sudden death underwater. Then there is an attempt on Laird's life. As a new storm of human violence gathers, Laird discovers that the Portuguese bay is hiding a powder keg of international proportions.

BILL KNOX

◆

SALVAGE JOB

Complete and Unabridged

LINFORD
Leicester

First published in the
United States of America
originally published as
'Salvage Job' by Michael Kirk

First Linford Edition
published 1997

British Library CIP Data

Bill, Knox, *1928* –
    Salvage job.—Large print ed.—
    Linford mystery library
    1. English fiction—20th century
    2. Large type books
    I. Title II. MacLeod, Robert, *1928* –
823.9'14 [F]

ISBN 0–7089–5022–1

Published by
F. A. Thorpe (Publishing) Ltd.
Anstey, Leicestershire

Set by Words & Graphics Ltd.
Anstey, Leicestershire
Printed and bound in Great Britain by
T. J. Press (Padstow) Ltd., Padstow, Cornwall

This book is printed on acid-free paper

For Meg MacLeod

Now this policy witnesseth that we, the Assurers, take upon ourselves the burden of this Assurance and promise and bind ourselves to the Assured, their Executors, Administrators, and Assigns for the true performance and fulfilment of the Contract contained in this Policy in consideration of the person or persons affecting this Policy promising to pay a premium at and after the Rate to be agreed.

(Extract from a present-day international marine insurance policy.)

1

THE man at the edge of the sea cliff lay flat, a .22 hunting rifle at his side, a pair of small, powerful binoculars in his grasp, his dark leather jacket and tan slacks blending with the coarse scrub and rock. The binoculars and his attention were focussed totally on the ship below.

Like some giant, stranded whale, the long, black rust-streaked hull of the oil tanker lay in the bright sunlight with her bow hard aground on the rocky shallows. From there, as the storm had left her, she protruded out across almost the entire width of the deep water channel which led from the sea to the sweep of a lagoon-like inner bay and the fishing town of Porto Esco.

There was no sign of activity on the tanker, but she wasn't deserted.

1

A launch, toy-sized by comparison, bobbed in the low waves which sparkled against her stem, where the bridge and funnel and living accommodations were crowded together. A line of washing, shirts and underclothes, flapped idly in the breeze between two lifeboat davits.

The man on the sea cliff eased his position slightly, the binoculars fixed on two men leaning on a deck rail near the tanker's bow. One was familiar to him, the other was the stranger he'd seen arrive by car in Porto Esco half an hour earlier. Satisfied, he lowered the binoculars, reached for the rifle, and wriggled back.

Once clear of the skyline he got up, tucked the binoculars away, cradled the rifle under the crook of his arm, and began walking.

Two minutes later he shot a running hare at fifty metres. The shot pleased him. Reaching the dead hare, he picked it up and stowed it in the game bag he had slung over one shoulder. Then he strode off in a straight line across the scrub and grass towards Porto Esco.

It had been curiosity which had brought him out. What he had to do for the moment was already done, what would follow would depend on others.

But he levered a fresh, long-nosed cartridge into the rifle as he walked. That was habit, the kind of habit that had nothing to do with hunting game.

* * *

The crack of the rifle shot reached the men on the tanker's bow as little more than a distant whip crack. Captain John Amos, master of the S.S. *Craig Michael*, Liberian registered, owned by the Anglo-Greek Antarah Line, currently wedded to a shoal of rock on the southern shore of Portugal, scowled briefly towards the sea cliff. He was a small, burly, dark man of Welsh blood and temperament, in his early forties.

Wearing an old roll-neck sweater and denim slacks, rope-soled sandals on his feet, be didn't look like the captain of a 50,000–ton dead weight tanker.

"So nobody blames me — fine," he said bitterly. His tanned face maintained its scowl and his dark eyes were bleak as he ran a hand through his short bristle of thinning grey hair. "But, man, do you think that's how people will remember it later? No chance. I'll be that damned Welshman Amos, the idiot who got his ship on the rocks."

"We all have our little problems, Captain," said Andrew Laird dryly, but with an underlying sympathy. "It could be worse."

It had been a lot worse for many. The storm had struck a week before on the first of April, All Fools' Day. A twisting Force Ten gale, it rampaged in from its birthplace in the Atlantic, carving a path across the Gulf of Cádiz, then surprising everyone by suddenly corkscrewing north and west again as

4

it touched the land barrier which acted like a bottleneck between the Atlantic and the Mediterranean.

Two small cargo ships had vanished with all hands in the terrible grey fury of those sixty-foot waves. Several other vessels, large and small, had limped into the nearest port. The badly damaged included a U.S. Navy destroyer which reached Lisbon with her pumps keeping her afloat and her upper works looking as if she'd been mauled by a berserk can opener. Ashore, along the coast line, there were houses without roofs, trees blown down, and livestock lying dead in the fields.

But just as suddenly the storm had passed, the sun shone down again, the wind became a slight breeze, and the sea returned to a gentle, rippling mirror of blue.

"The old bitch stayed intact," admitted Captain Amos. "Forty feet of her keel clawed as raw as an itchy backside on those rocks but not as much as a trickle of water coming in — yes, I'll go along with you, Laird. We were damned lucky."

Andrew Laird nodded and looked along the seven-hundred-foot length of deck to the distant string of drying laundry. Twice the length of a football field, one hundred feet wide, the *Craig Michael* had been a giant among ships when she had been built twenty years earlier. She still looked big — very big, even if she had become dwarfed by the modern supertankers, where 250,000 tons was commonplace.

And the way she'd survived the storm was close to a miracle.

Andrew Laird looked around, the dry geographical detail in the Clanmore Alliance report file coming to life in terms of land and sea, shape and colour.

The long sea cliff headland of Cabo Esco, forty kilometres west of the Portuguese frontier with Spain, guarded a bay shaped like a twisted dumbbell. For four months the *Craig Michael* had been part of the scenery in

6

the outer bay, lying empty and moored in deep water, only Captain Amos and a tiny maintenance team aboard. Work was in short supply for tankers her size — the super-tanker age had made them almost an embarrassment to owners; there were others like her waiting in bays and estuaries throughout the world for voyages that seldom came or often meant just a final trip to a shipbreaking yard.

Five nights earlier, when the storm had hit, it had come angling into the bay against all normal patterns. Huge seas had ripped loose the *Craig Michael*'s giant anchors. Without power, helpless, the vast steel hull had been swept up towards the channel that led to the inner bay — and there she had struck.

Struck and stayed the rest of that long night. Daylight and the dying storm had revealed the stranded giant to the fishermen who came out from Porto Esco. The *Craig Michael* almost blocked their gateway to the sea — almost, but not quite. A fishing boat could still squeeze past her stern. The real marvel was that she had survived as a ship and that her watchmen crew were safe.

"Twenty years at sea and the first time a ship of mine grounds it has to be this way," said Amos as if reading Laird's thoughts. He leaned his small, squat frame against the rail and considered his visitor with the sensible caution any ship's master reserved for the marine insurance world. "Hardly decent, is it?"

Andrew Laird gave a faint grin. Below them, the rippling wavelets lapped gently against the *Craig Michael*'s hull and he could see the rocky ledges which lay below the clear water. The ledges and their occasional clumps of quivering green weed seemed alive with darting schools of tiny fish. The afternoon sun was warm on his back, relaxing his travel-weary muscles. For the moment, though he didn't think Amos would appreciate it, the world seemed reasonably pleasant.

Over medium height and stocky, with a muscular build, his dark, thick hair prematurely grey at the temples, Andrew Laird was close to his thirtieth birthday. Grey-green eyes and a nose which had been broken at some time gave him a face strangers might call hard-set — until they saw the way his mouth could pucker into an easy, almost boyish smile. He also had long, strong-fingered hands and a voice which still held a wisp of his native Scottish accent.

Amos's inspection had taken in all of these things. He noted, too, the casual cut of Laird's tan gaberdine suit, which he wore with a light blue shirt, knitted blue tie, and tan moccasin shoes. More interesting, his visitor's wrists both showed the tip of stylised tattoo markings and the plaited leather belt at his waist had a distinctive seaman's buckle.

"Ever sail on tankers, mister?" asked Amos.

"I've got sea time," admitted Laird.

"But never tankers — "

"I wondered." Amos nodded, satisfied, feeling more at ease. "All right, we can talk the same language. What happens now as far as you're concerned?"

Laird shrugged. "We've already got a surveyor's report and a diving survey. I add my own report to head office, and the paperwork is tidied with your owners. The final claim won't be settled until you've refloated and all the bills are in but I don't see too many problems."

"She'll refloat easily enough," said Amos. "I go along with the surveyor's report. Wait ten days until high water at the next spring tide, when there's an extra few feet of water under the hull, and she'll come off on her own. Give me a couple of decent-sized salvage tugs and a tow master who knows his job and we'll have her back at anchor."

"No sense in trying before then," said Laird.

"You mean who's pushing for an

out-of-work tanker," said Amos. Then he hauled an old-fashioned pocket watch from his denims, glanced at the time, then stowed the watch away again. "Anything else you want to see, mister?"

"Not this visit," Laird assured him.

"Good." Amos hesitated. "Uh — you know I've got my wife living aboard?"

Laird nodded. Officers' wives were often carried by tankers at sea. It was even more natural and human when a ship was at a long-term mooring.

"There's usually coffee on the go about now," suggested Amos. "She likes meeting visitors, unless you're in a rush — "

"I'm not," said Laird. His curiosity was mildly roused and though a cool beer would have been a better offer it also mattered that he built a friendly relationship with the *Craig Michael*'s master. "You lead, Captain."

There were two pedal cycles propped incongruously against an inspection hatch close by. Most tankers carried a few for easy transport along their vast expanses of deck space. They climbed aboard the bikes and pedalled along, the tyres purring on the steel deck plates. On the way, a lanky, fair-haired man in overalls who was working at another of the inspection hatches waved a greeting.

"Jody Cruft, our bo'sun," explained Amos as they passed and pedalled on. "He's tank-checking — one of our routine chores."

They reached the shade of the *Craig Michael*'s high aft bridge structure, dismounted, left the cycles beside a companionway door, and went through into a large, cool day cabin. Another man was already there, lounging back in a chair and nursing a mug of coffee. He nodded, while a red-haired woman came forward to greet them with a smile.

"My wife, Mary," said Amos. "Mary, this is Andrew Laird. For an insurance man he seems reasonably human."

Mary Amos laughed and shook

hands. She had a freckled, raw-boned but still attractive face and was in her mid-forties. She wore what looked like one of her husband's tropical shirts with blue shorts, and the red hair was tied back. Although she was in bare feet, she stood two or three inches taller than her husband.

"I've got my orders about you, Mr. Laird," she said cheerfully. "Treat him kindly till we find out what we're dealing with."

"Let me know when you decide," said Laird.

"When *he* decides," she corrected, with a glance at her husband. "How long are you here for?"

"Just long enough to get my report sorted out — a couple of days." Laird sensed what she really wanted to know. "I don't see any problems. Certainly no blame."

"Good." This time, the glance she gave her husband held relief. She gestured towards the percolator and mugs on a sideboard. "How do you

13

like your coffee?"

He asked for black. As she turned to get it, a sound came from the other man in the cabin, who hadn't moved from his chair. He was a bald, bean-pole thin figure in a faded vest and grubby white overalls, considerably older than Amos.

"Maybe no blame, but no medals," he said flatly. "The owners wouldn't ha' wept tears if we'd ended up a wreck. They'd ha' grabbed the insurance cheque."

"Meet our resident cynic," said Captain Amos. "Andy Dawson, our engineer."

"Anybody going to tell me I'm wrong?" asked Dawson. "Sure, the *Craig Michael* is a good enough ship. But who wants her — or us?"

"Shut up, Andy," said Mary Amos softly, coming back and handing Laird a filled coffee mug. "Either that, or go and play with your oilcan somewhere. I mean it."

Dawson scowled at her for a moment,

14

then shrugged, rose, and put down his coffee mug.

"I've things to do anyway," he said. Then he left, giving Laird a curt nod.

"He's a surly devil at times," sighed Amos apologetically. Bringing out a pack of cigarettes, he flipped one across to his wife, then offered them to Laird. "Go ahead — we're in a Smoking Zone. There aren't too many of them on a tanker."

Laird took a cigarette, accepted a light from Amos in his turn, then sipped his coffee.

"You've three men aboard with you, right?" he began.

Amos nodded. "Dawson, Jody Cruft, the bo'sun — he's Dutch — and Cheung, our utility man. Cheung is from Hong Kong via Liverpool." He frowned across at his wife. "Where's Cheung anyway?"

"Down talking to the boatman who brought Mr. Laird out," she answered, settling into a chair, curling her bare feet under her. "Friendly relations — "

"That won't do any harm." Amos drew on his cigarette and grimaced at Laird. "We aren't too popular with the Porto Esco fishermen for what we've done to the channel. They can still squeeze past, but don't be surprised if some try to hit you for a compensation claim."

"Like they all want new boats?" Laird grinned. "They can try." Something else was on his mind. "You told me your bo'sun was tank-testing. Didn't you have a full tank-cleaning before you laid up?"

"Yes, but in my book that's not a total guarantee," said Amos. His dark features were furrowed. "I saw a tanker blow up just once, mister. That was enough. I'll take it you know the basics — in this game, things are safest when your tanks are full and most dangerous when they're empty."

Laird nodded. Petroleum vapour was the lurking, unseen, enemy. Even a cleaned tank declared gas-free could only be positively free at the time of its test — and petroleum vapour might still return from a forgotten pump or valve, be released by a simple disturbance of loose scale on the tank plates, or recur a dozen other ways. Petroleum vapour mixed with air in a confined space amounted to a flash-point bomb, the smallest spark enough to act as a total detonator.

"You don't take chances," he said softly.

"Would you?" Amos grinned. "For a start, Mary looks like hell in black. So I stick to my own routine — and that includes a gas reading from every tank every day."

Andrew Laird considered the small, burly man with a new respect. To be stuck four months in a backwater anchorage and still maintain a steady disciplined routine was no everyday achievement. But one other aspect of the *Craig Michael* puzzled him. Now seemed as good a time as any to ask.

"You were master on the *Craig*

Michael before she was — well, parked down here?"

Amos nodded. "I've had her for five years. She was my first command."

"Not many owners would leave a captain and three other qualified men — "

"Two," corrected Amos. "Cheung's a good all-rounder, that's all."

"Two," accepted Laird. "But you're aboard, you're expensive. The regular thing would be to put a couple of pensioners aboard as watchmen and leave it at that."

Amos glanced at his wife, who gave a dry laugh which held little humour.

"The Antarah Line don't waste money, Mr. Laird," she said. "Blend a bunch of English and Greeks together and they could teach the Mafia a thing or two about tough business operations. But they've a reason."

Amos nodded. "Charter work — that's the name of the game. My job is to keep the *Craig Michael* on forty-eight hours' readiness. If anybody needs a tanker in

18

a hurry, maybe another tanker outfit with a sudden problem, then Antarah Lines jump in. They'll fly out a crew grabbed from the union pool." He made no attempt to sound enthusiastic. "They've had two other tankers laid up on the same basis, one in the U.K. and one in South America, and both are working again. Our turn will come, I suppose — and emergency charters pay well over the odds."

"I didn't imagine it was a charity operation." Laird glanced at his watch. It was near to 4 P.M. and the Clanmore office in London would be closing in about an hour. He finished the coffee, laid down the mug, and rose. "Thanks for showing me round, Captain. I'll head back to Porto Esco now, but I'll come out again tomorrow."

"We could have fixed you up with a spare cabin aboard," said Amos, getting to his feet. "We still can if — "

"I've a room booked and waiting," said Laird. "It's at a place called the Pousada Pico."

19

"You'll be all right there. It's the local tourist inn — if Porto Esco has ever had a tourist." Mary Amos squirmed round in her chair and gave her husband an amused glance. "And some people say the Pico has its own attractions, don't they, John?"

Amos grinned but didn't take the bait. Then as he went towards the door with Laird, he stopped beside a notice. It said: 'You Are Leaving a Smoking Zone', and there was an ashtray underneath. They stubbed out their cigarettes before they went on.

Back on the open deck, the bright sunlight reflecting from the water in a way that almost dazzled, Laird nearly collided with a figure about to go in. It was Jody Cruft, the lanky, fair-haired bo'sun, and he had a heavy meter case on a sling over one shoulder.

"All correct, Jody?" asked Amos.

"Clear readings from all tanks, Cap'n," said Cruft, and vanished in through the companionway.

The *Craig Michael*'s master walked

with Laird in silence until they reached the ladder that led down to the waiting launch. The boatman, a bronzed figure wearing just trousers and an old cap, glanced up, saw them, and said something to the man in overalls who was sitting with him on the engine hatch. The second man nodded and came clambering up. Small and slight, with jet black hair, Cheung the utility man showed Amos the small net bag of oranges he was carrying, then ambled off along the deck.

"He's in the barter game," said Amos. "Paint and ship's stores for fresh fruit and vegetables — he knows I know, but what the hell?" He stuck out his hand. "Tomorrow, then."

"In the morning," promised Laird. He shook hands with Amos, climbed down the ladder, and as he stepped into the launch the boatman was already casting off the line which held them to the tanker's ladder.

Ancient engine clattering and a stink of exhaust in the air, the launch swung away from the vast black hull and began to head up the dog-leg channel. For a moment, Laird looked back at the bulk of the stranded tanker, then turned, found himself a seat on the thwarts, and settled back while the old boat grumbled on through the quiet water and the inner lagoon of Cabo Esco bay gradually opened up before him.

The tide was out and the result left the inner bay shaped like a mile wide saddle with dried-out shallows to the north and east. To the west, Porto Esco was a long, thin line of white buildings with a small forest of fishing boat masts beside its grey stone quayside. Further north, he could see the hump of a road bridge over a river which joined the bay — he'd driven over the bridge on his way in. That left an odd, isolated cluster of buildings to the northeast, where the deep water extended like the pommel of the saddle between the two low-tide stretches of sand and gravel.

Mustering his rusty Portuguese, he

pointed and asked above the noise of the engine, "What's over there?"

"Senhor?" The boatman looked puzzled till Laird pointed again, then understood. "For old ships, ver' old ships — where they die."

"A shipbreaking yard?" Laird raised an interesting eyebrow. "*Por favor*, who owns it?"

"That depends who you ask." The boatman spat cheerfully downwind and across the launch, the result clearing the scarred gunwale by a hairsbreadth. "Some will still say the Workers Council, others that it is Senhor da Costa and his friend — me, I don't know an' don't care."

Laird didn't follow up. Foreigners were welcome in Portugal. But they showed sense if they didn't ask too many questions in a country still recovering from a more or less bloodless revolution which had sent it lurching far to the left, then back to a delicate political balancing act called democracy. He glanced down at a

23

small locker lying open beside the boatman's feet and fought down a grin. An unopened can of ship's issue dried milk was lying among a clutter of rusty tools and dirty oil rags.

There was always an angle, whatever the politics.

★ ★ ★

They nosed in against the quayside at Porto Esco a few minutes later, rubbing the old car tyre fenders of a couple of fishing boats in the process. Laird paid off the boatman, climbed a flight of worn steps to the quayside, and walked across to where he'd left the hired yellow Simca he'd driven over from Faro airport.

Then as he caught sight of the car he slowed.

The bulky sergeant of *policia* leaning against the radiator grille had his hands in his pockets and a small, thin cigar smouldering between his lips. He saw Laird, flipped the cigar away, brushed a trace of ash from his grey-blue uniform, and gave a weary salute as he levered himself upright.

"Your car, senhor?" he asked.

Laird sniffed the air as he nodded. The sergeant used a powerful brand of aftershave. He also had a face like a piece of rough-carved wood, a thin black moustache, and the start of a middle-aged paunch.

"And you have your *passaporte*?" One thumb hooked into the leather belt which sagged under the weight of a heavy baton, a holstered automatic, and a separate ammunition clip-holder; the man waited impassively till Laird brought out his passport and handed it over. He flicked through its pages with a casual air, then returned it with a nod. "*Obrigado*. Now, we have a small problem."

"Like what, Sergeant?" asked Laird politely, tucking the passport away again.

"Your car." A large, highly polished boot gently tapped against the nearest

25

tyre. "No cars can be parked on this quay. And even in Porto Esco one should not leave luggage in a car and the doors unlocked."

Swearing softly under his breath, Laird opened the driver's door and looked inside the car. His travel bag was still lying on the rear seat, but the plastic carrier load of duty-free liquor and cigarettes he'd purchased on the flight out from London that morning was gone. He sighed, knowing he had locked the doors, knowing that the average car lock didn't stand a chance against any passing layabout with a jigger key or a suitable piece of stiff wire.

"Senhor?" The bulky policeman strolled round to join him. "Is anything missing?"

Slowly, Laird shook his head. He'd learned the hard way in plenty of places that it seldom paid to make waves unless it really mattered.

The man's heavy face took on a slightly benevolent air. "Next time, you might not be so lucky. Ah — you are staying in Porto Esco?"

"At the Pousada Pico, once I find it."

"*Em frente* . . . it is along the quayside, past these boats." The benevolence continued. "As you have just arrived, we will forget the matter of illegal parking." He paused. "My name is Manuel Ramos. Most evenings I look in at the bar of the Pico just before sundown — "

"Then maybe I can buy you a drink," said Laird straight-faced and on cue.

"*Obrigado*, Senhor Laird." Sergeant Ramos took a hitch on his harness belt and saluted again. "*Adeus.* Enjoy your stay."

He ambled off, the baton joggling against one hip, satisfaction in his stride. Wryly, wondering how often Sergeant Ramos had to reach into his own pocket for drinking money, Laird got into the Simca and set it moving as he'd been directed.

The Pousado Pico was only about a minute's drive along the shore road, which had houses and shops on one side and a line of small craft, mostly fishing boats, moored to the low wall which divided it from the sea. The tourist inn was a plain, flat-roofed three-storey building with white stucco walls, narrow, shuttered windows, and a faded sun awning which sheltered a few pavement tables where a handful of customers sat drinking.

A signboard directed him round to a small courtyard at the rear, empty apart from some buzzing flies. He parked the Simca, took his travel bag, and went through a side door into the gloom of the *pousada*'s lobby. It had a cool terrazzo floor and as he crossed towards the small, deserted reception desk a woman emerged from an office at the rear.

"Senhor?" She was middle-aged, probably in her fifties, but slim, smart, and sharp-eyed. Her black hair streaked lightly with grey was cut in an almost boyish style to frame a still attractive face and she wore a narrow black skirt with a patterned shirt blouse. "Can I help you?"

He nodded. "You've a reservation for Andrew Laird — I hope."

"*Sim* . . . it was cabled." She pushed the *pousada*'s register across. While he signed, she selected a key from the rack behind her and laid it on the counter. "Room 22. The stairway is to your right."

Laird took the key and his travel bag, climbed two fights of stairs, and found Room 22 almost facing him at the top with the door lying ajar. He pushed it open, then simultaneously felt the wood collide with something solid and heard a startled, muffled yelp of protest.

Going in, he stared at the rear view of a distinctly feminine pair of tight blue denim jeans wriggling out from under the bed behind the door.

"Sorry," he began hastily. "I thought — "

The rest of the girl emerged and she scrambled to her feet indignantly, rubbing her rear. Laird couldn't stop the grin which slid across his face and the girl's indignation melted, giving way to a rueful grimace.

"My fault," she agreed in English. Her voice was crisp but friendly, with no trace of an accent. "Senhor Laird?"

"Andrew Laird," he nodded. "I was told Room 22."

"You've found it," she said cheerfully. "I don't normally dive under stranger's beds, but I dropped this and it rolled." She showed him a small black screwdriver. "I'd just finished changing the plug on your bedside light. It should work now."

"You're the electrician?" asked Laird, amused, and put down his travel bag.

He liked what he saw. The girl, almost his own height and beautifully proportioned, had long, tawny hair and a smooth, bronzed skin. Her striking looks were emphasised by high cheekbones and a wide, generous mouth; the denim jeans were topped by a thin red and white striped sweater, and her feet were in red leather sandals.

"I'm Katarina Gunn — Kati for short."

"English?" he asked.

"English father, Portuguese mother — there's a lot of us about." She chuckled. "Here, I'm just family, helping out. Who was on the desk downstairs?"

"A woman in her fifties," said Laird. "Dark-haired, slim build, and she knew what she was doing."

"She's my aunt — my mother's sister," nodded Kati Gunn. "Senhora da Costa — she's a widow and she owns this place."

Laird raised an eyebrow. "Any relation to the da Costa who runs that little shipbreaking yard across the bay?"

"That's her son." The girl gave a slight frown. "My cousin José — do you know him?"

"No, I just heard the name." Laird switched to something that interested him more. "Do you live here?"

"I visit," she corrected. "I live in Lisbon, but right now I've got some holiday time." Her hazel eyes considered him with some curiosity. "Your reservation was cabled from London. Are you here because of the tanker in the channel?"

"The insurance side of it." Laird had a sudden thought. "One person I want to meet is a local diver called Jorges Soller — he did an underwater survey on the tanker's hull. Any idea where I'll find him?"

"I'll show you." She beckoned Laird over to the window, which looked out from the front of the *pousada* across the bay. Opening the window, she leaned on the sill in a way which did alarming things with her thin sweater and pointed down, across the street, to the line of boats at the water's edge. "Just watch for a boat called the *Juhno* coming in — he usually moors her near here and he lives aboard."

"Where will he be now?" asked Laird.

"Diving for clam shells somewhere — he sells them to the tourist shops." She glanced round. "I can get a message to him when he comes back, if you want."

"Thanks. Just say I want to talk to him." Laird's eyes rested on one of the boats. A low, fast cabin launch painted dark blue, it bobbed lightly in the middle of the line of fishing craft. He could just read the name *Mama Isabel* lettered in white at her bow. "Who owns the glamour job?"

"My cousin José," she said dryly. "He named her after his mother — José keeps on her good side when he can." Then she turned away from the window. "I'd better do the same. I'm supposed to earn my keep while I'm here."

"Will you be around later?" asked Laird.

She smiled, nodded, and went out, closing the door.

Laird shut the window, peeled off his jacket, and dropped it on a chair. Then he flopped down on the bed for a moment and glanced around the room. It was spotlessly clean with the usual pieces of basic furniture and a small washroom and shower. Listening to the low murmur of an occasional passing car in the street below, his mind straying again to Kati Gunn, he decided he'd landed up in worse places.

A wicker basket filled with fruit had been left beside the telephone on his bedside table. He helped himself to a peach, took a couple of bites, then lifted the telephone. He heard it buzz at the *pousada*'s switchboard for a moment, then Senhora da Costa's voice came on the line. He resisted the temptation to call her Mama Isabel, explained he wanted a call to London, gave the number, and hung up.

He had finished the peach by the

time the call came through. The girl on the Clanmore Alliance switchboard in London sounded bored as she connected him to Osgood Morris, the marine claims department's general manager.

"So you're still working for us?" came Morris's querulous voice over the line. There was a pause and a sniff. "I take it you're sitting in some bar, enjoying a drink?"

"Two drinks and a girl," countered Laird cheerfully. "Don't be jealous, Osgood. It's bad for your image."

"Do you realise I've had the chairman's personal secretary on twice this afternoon, just asking if I'd heard from you?"

Laird grinned. Osgood Morris might not, as rumour declared, polish the chairman's shoes and treasure his discarded cigar butts. But he certainly tried hard to build up points with an eye to some possible future on the Clanmore Alliance board.

"All right," he said. "I've been on

the *Craig Michael*, I've talked to the master, and everything seems on the line — just like the surveyor's report, just like you hoped."

"Perhaps." Morris wore habitual caution like a bullet-proof vest. "And she'll refloat without damage?"

"If they wait, like the survey report suggested — the captain certainly goes along with the idea, and it looks feasible." Laird eased himself into a more comfortable position on the bed. "I've still to talk to the diver who made the underwater check, but if we're lucky it'll just come down to some clever work by a couple of salvage tugs on the next spring tide."

"Yes." Morris's voice faded, then came back. "Unfortunately, the owners — ah — are restless. We had the Antarah Lines in touch today, hinting. They also advised they've hired a salvage expert in Lisbon to make an independent report. You can expect him in Porto Esco tomorrow."

"Why? What's going on?" Laird

propped himself up and blinked at the receiver. "Osgood, that damned tanker has been rusting at her anchor chains for months — "

"They're Anglo-Greek," said Morris. "But the Antarah Lines represent a lot of premium income to Clanmore Alliance, as the chairman reminded me. We don't want to — ah — upset them needlessly by being awkward at this stage. You understand?"

Laird sighed. "Look, if anyone tries to haul that tanker off by brute force and things go wrong you won't just have a brand-new wreck. You'll have a totally blocked channel and half the fishermen in Portugal queuing to sue for damages."

"I know." Osgood Morris sounded ill at the thought. "The risk insurance on that hull is several million pounds; we may have to take a firm line with them later, but — ah — for now you'll give their salvage expert courtesy and cooperation. You understand?"

"No, but I'll try," said Laird.

"What's his name?"

"I've got it here. He's captain of an ocean-going tug and apparently an experienced tow master." Morris rustled papers for a moment. "Yes — he's a Captain Harry Novak."

The name hit Andrew Laird like a harsh jolt from over a gap of years. He swore softly and pungently while the sunlight pouring into his room seemed to take on a sudden shade of grey.

"You know him?" asked Morris.

"I know him," said Laird slowly. "He's a prize bastard."

And an all-round hard man. Harry Novak knew his job, even his enemies gave him that much. Nobody knew what his friends said. Nobody had ever come across one.

"Well, I'm afraid that's going to be your problem," said Morris. "Call me tomorrow."

He hung up before Laird could reply. Laird held his receiver a moment longer, tight-lipped, his mind bitter with memories. Then, suddenly, just before the line went dead, he heard the murmur of a voice, then a click.

Someone who had been listening had just closed a switchboard key. Almost certainly at the Pousada Pico switchboard, and they'd been clumsy about it.

He shrugged, not caring for the moment. Getting up from the bed he went over to the window, rested his hands on the sill, and stared out at the boats and the bay.

Harry Novak — the man was a memory from the past, the kind Andrew Laird could have done without. A memory, mainly, of the night the bullying tug master had whimpered like a child while his brand-new radio operator had stitched a gash down one whole side of Novak's face. The gash had been carved by a berserk deck hand using a broken bottle; Laird had stitched it with a blunt needle and Novak, asking no questions about how a radioman came to have medical skills, had treated Laird with a grudging respect from that moment on.

Smiling slightly, Laird glanced down at his hands on the sill and the stylised tattoo marks which showed on his wrists and ran on under his shirt cuffs. The Chinese dragon which clawed on his left arm and the foul anchor with a chain on his right arm had been done one harebrained night in Hong Kong — the same night he'd ended up with a broken nose.

Before Novak. When Andrew Laird, sheep farmer's son from the Scottish Highlands and recent final year medical student with a chance of winning his class gold medal, had used the sea as an escape route from a reality he didn't regret.

There hadn't been police action because there wasn't enough evidence. The woman had been his mother, his crime had been refusing to go on watching and doing nothing while she suffered without hope. He'd met sympathy and understanding, but in medicine the real crime was being caught — and the doors had closed in his face.

He'd signed on his first ship as a deck hand. Deep sea, then another ship and another voyage, which had included Hong Kong. Restless, he'd trained as a radio operator after that. Which had led him to his first ocean-going salvage tug and a few months with Harry Novak.

He'd been on his third ocean-going tug, with a friendly skipper, when a green-eyed girl with copper hair had made him decide to quit the sea and start in the marine insurance game.

Her name had been Maureen. His discharge pay had bought the engagement ring. Platinum with two diamonds and a sapphire and she'd pawned it three months later for an air ticket to Canada. Going off with another man and posting him the pawn ticket as her good-bye message.

"The hell with it," he said softly, still standing at the window.

He liked working for Clanmore

Alliance, he could even get along with Osgood Morris most of the time. If there was any kind of clash coming with Harry Novak, he might almost enjoy that too.

Lighting a cigarette, he took a long draw on it and was turning away from the window when a figure in the street below caught his eyes. A tall, black-haired man wearing tan slacks and a leather jacket was striding across to where the blue hull of the *Mama Isabel* bobbed beside the sea wall.

The man stooped, cast off the launch's mooring line, stepped aboard, and went into the cockpit. The engine fired with a shimmer of exhaust, the *Mama Isabel* eased stern first out from the wall, then stopped for a moment while the black-haired man gave a wave to someone ashore. Then he swung the wheel, the launch engine bellowed, and the blue hull curved away, gathering speed, building a white wake as she headed across the bay.

Curious, Laird opened his window

and leaned out. He was in time to see Senhora da Costa disappearing through a street door into the Pico.

Closing the window again, he grimaced. Porto Esco had reason to be interested in what was happening to the tanker which almost blocked its channel. José da Costa, with his little shipbreaking yard, probably had his own stake — and an edge on most people if his mother allowed him to eavesdrop at the *pousada*'s switchboard.

Turning away, Laird opened his travel bag and started to unpack with a sad thought for his stolen duty-free liquor and cigarettes. Then he heard a knock on the door and it opened.

"Me," said Kati Gunn briskly, coming in. She laid some clean towels on the bed. "I forgot these — Mama Isabel says sorry. Oh, and I've some news for you about Jorges Soller. He'll be later back than usual — according to Cousin José, he's down along the coast doing a diving job for someone."

"There's no rush," said Laird. "I saw José taking his launch out. She certainly moves."

The tawny-haired girl nodded without enthusiasm. "He'll tell you it's the fastest boat on the coast — except for the sports boats at the marinas around Faro."

"How's business at his shipbreaking yard?" asked Laird casually.

"I wouldn't know," said Kati Gunn. "But José doesn't exactly overwork himself."

"So the tanker won't worry him too much?" probed Laird.

"He hasn't been howling about it so far. The local fishermen are the ones who're making a noise." She grinned and went back out.

As the door closed, Laird turned back to his unpacking. He finished, then spotted the bed lamp plug still lying loose on the end of its flex.

Stooping, he pushed the plug into its socket.

There was a bang, the plug blasted

out again, and a small curl of blue smoke came for a moment from its blackened plastic.

He sighed and shook his head.

Whatever Kati Gunn's talents, she was one hell of a poor electrician.

2

IT had been a long day and Andrew Laird yielded to temptation. He sprawled back on the bed for a five-minute nap and woke almost an hour later with the sunlight already beginning to fade outside his room. He could smell cooking and heard the distant clatter of pans coming from the *pousada*'s kitchen while he showered, shaved, and treated himself to a change of shirt.

Feeling fresh and clean again, he left the room and went down to the lobby. A sign pointed the way to the bar and he was heading in that direction when he heard his name called and stopped.

"*Boa tarde*, Senhor Laird." Isabel da Costa's small high-heeled shoes clicked briskly across the cool terrazzo floor as she came towards him. The tall, black-haired man Laird had spotted earlier followed behind her at a more leisurely pace, smiling slightly. Even if Laird hadn't been told before it would have been easy to guess who he was. Wiry, tanned, and aged about thirty, José da Costa had his mother's sharp eyes and fine-boned features — and, briskly, Isabel da Costa got to the point. "This is my son José. He is most anxious to meet you."

"I've already heard about him." Laird shook hands with da Costa, who was still in the same outfit of leather jacket and slacks. "Then I saw you take off in your boat. She looks fairly fast."

"*Sim.*" Da Costa had a dry, lazy voice but seemed pleased. She's the fastest hull on this part of the coast. But that was just a round-trip errand across the bay — come out as a passenger sometime and see what she really can do."

"First chance I get," said Laird.

"Your room is comfortable enough, Senhor?" interrupted Isabel da Costa.

"If you need anything — "

"It's just fine," he said. "No problems."

"You're a welcome guest here, Senhor Laird," said da Costa. "That applies to anyone likely to help us get rid of that damned tanker from our channel."

"Salvage isn't my business," said Laird. "I'm only involved on the insurance side."

"*Entendo* . . . yes, I understand." Da Costa smiled slightly. "But what you say still matters when it comes to decisions."

"Not always," said Laird cautiously. "If you're talking business, I know about your firm. But — "

"That?" The smile became a grin. "Senhor, my little Companhia Tecnico is not looking for work from you. To ask us to help refloat that ship would be like asking a sardine to help a whale — something to laugh about."

"I wouldn't have put it quite like that," said Laird.

"But that's what was on your mind,"

said da Costa. "No, I want to give you a friendly warning. Particularly if you're on your way to the bar for a drink."

"Something wrong with your prices?" asked Laird.

Isabel da Costa didn't look amused, but her son chuckled.

"Nothing like that. The barman even keeps his thumb out of the glass. But at this hour most of our customers are fishermen. They may want to talk about compensation claims."

"I'm paid to listen," said Laird. "Haven't you had any thoughts in that direction?"

"Not yet," said da Costa. "So far the *Craig Michael* has made no difference to us. But soon we will have a load of steel scrap due to be shipped out and if there was delay — " He shrugged, his sharp eyes watching closely. "Still, maybe after tomorrow we will know more."

"Tomorrow?"

"When this salvage man, Captain

Novak, comes from Lisbon," said da Costa. He stuck his hands in the pockets of his leather jacket. "He telephoned and chartered a boat from me — he says he will be bringing his own diver with him, for another survey."

"Captain Novak knows his business." The diver was news to Laird, but he didn't show it. "He may have some fresh ideas."

If Novak had, Laird didn't want to imagine them. But da Costa seemed satisfied and his mother was making slightly impatient noises at his side.

"*Venho*, Mama Isabel," soothed da Costa. "I'm coming." He explained to Laird: "She has some tax forms to fill out — I promised I'd help, which was a mistake."

"Anything to do with tax is a mistake," agreed Laird solemnly.

"True," said da Costa. "But it has to be done. I'll see you again — and if my Companhia Tecnico can help in any small way, let me know. We take anyone's money."

He shepherded his mother back into the little office. Laird continued on his way, still thinking about Novak, puzzling over the news that he was bringing a diver. The bar was on the other side of a beaded curtain down a short passageway and he went in, then sat at a vacant table.

The only vacant table, he realised — and the low buzz of conversation that had been going on had died away with his arrival. All that was left was a soft moan of *fado* music coming from a radio mounted on one wall.

It was a small bar, not much more than half a dozen tables and a countertop, the plain walls decorated with old magazine pin-up pictures and a few faded bullfight posters. The windows looked out towards the bay, the pavement tables outside were empty, dusk greying its way across the water. But there were a score or so of customers inside, most of them fishermen by their dress. They seemed to be waiting for something to happen and the white-coated barman, studiously ignoring him, was making a vigorous pretence of polishing a glass with an old cloth.

Then, as he'd expected, it happened. Two men rose from one of the tables and crossed purposefully towards him. Both wore frayed, crumpled overalls and old, cutdown sea boots. The smaller, who was scrawny, middle-aged, and unshaven, had a greasy old felt hat on his head. His companion, a younger, paunchy individual with a fat, pock-marked face, was the one who did the talking.

"You are from the people who insure the tanker ship?" he demanded loudly.

Easing back in his chair, Laird nodded.

"Then, *por favor*, we have to talk to you." The man cleared his throat and glanced back at the other tables for support. "As elected representatives of the fishermen of Porto Esco — "

"Elected?"

"It was agreed, senhor," said the smaller man. "Miguel an' I asked aroun' and — "

A quick scowl and a nudge from his companion silenced him. Then the paunchy figure began again, giving an appealing gesture with both hands.

"Every day that ship stays across the Cabo Esco channel we lose money. Our boats cannot sail or risk danger, the fish are not caught — "

"Your families grow hungry?" suggested Laird.

"*Sim*, it is so." He beamed agreement.

"So you reckon you've a claim against the tanker?" asked Laird in the same mild, understanding voice.

Both men nodded.

"Then I'll tell you what I think," said Laird. He ended the pretence, considering the pair with a sudden, cutting edge to his words. "I don't mind a try-on, if it's a good one. But I've heard better stories from a backward two-year-old. Forget it."

"Senhor — " The smaller man

was startled, but he didn't go on. Their audience looked bewildered and stayed quiet while the low *fado* music continued to grind in the background.

"Let me give you and your friends some free advice," said Laird. "If you're looking for money, get off your backsides and try working for it. That channel isn't blocked to any fishing boat I've seen around here — and there's no way you'll find any insurance handout coming along."

A growl came from the fat man. Shoving his friend aside, he lurched forward.

But Laird wasn't there. Skidding his chair back, sidestepping as he rose, he easily evaded a wild, haymaking blow — and the man's clumsy rush sent him tripping over the chair. He went sprawling on the wooden floor with a crash and hauled himself up cursing. An empty bottle was lying on the next table, and the man grabbed it, swinging it back like a club.

Laird tensed, but suddenly the man

seemed to freeze. Looking past Laird, licking his lips uneasily, he let the bottle come down to his side.

"*Multo obrigado*, Miguel," came a sardonic growl from the rear.

Glancing round, Laird saw Sergeant Ramos standing at the curtained doorway which led from the *pousada* lobby. He ambled forward, thumbs hooked in his leather belt, his craggy face only mildly disapproving. He nodded politely to Laird, looked almost lazily around the barroom, then brought his attention back to the two 'elected representatives' in front of him.

"Out," he said curtly, thumbing towards the street door.

Sullenly, the two fishermen obeyed. The man called Miguel was still carrying the empty bottle as they left. The door slammed shut behind them, the bartender relaxed and turned up the radio's volume, and the other customers began talking again.

"Nice timing," said Laird with some relief. "Sergeant, I was going to buy you a drink. How about right now?"

Sergeant Ramos smiled and took a chair opposite while Laird settled down again. A snap of Ramos's fingers brought the barman hurrying over with a bottle and two glasses.

"Local brandy, Senhor Laird," said Ramos cheerfully, waving the barman away and doing the pouring. "Good stuff — you should like it. They — ah — will put the bottle on your bill."

Laird nodded, lifted the glass in a silent toast, and took a sip. The brandy burned, but he'd tasted worse. Sergeant Ramos's method was a straight swallow which emptied his glass; then he poured himself a refill.

"I looked in to see Senhora da Costa," he explained. "She told me. Were these two pieces of garbage trying to get money from you?"

"Making out they had a claim against the tanker," said Laird. "The fat one got upset about things."

"They are *pequeno* — of no importance," said Ramos. "All they do is hang around the boats, stirring up trouble." He sucked his teeth reflectively. "I would have them behind bars except that my *posto da policia* would have to be fumigated afterwards."

"What about the others here?" Laird gestured at the crowded tables, where drinking and talk had begun again.

"Your real fishermen — most of them, anyway." Ramos took another long swallow from his glass. "Simple enough to be talked into most things — and why not? Everyone knows that insurance companies have fat moneybags. But you killed the idea so now they'll forget it." He paused. "When little incidents like this happen, I have a philosophy — sit back, let others see you are watching, but do nothing."

"Does it work?" asked Laird dryly.

Ramos shrugged. "Senhor Laird, in Portugal a man has to remember that anything can happen. Or that is how it has been lately — politics. Should I lock up a man today when he might be the damn mayor of Porto Esco tomorrow?"

"In insurance, we call that all-risks cover." Laird kept down a smile at the basic logic. His opinion of Ramos was gradually changing — the bulky, stone-faced figure in uniform wouldn't have won any 'Cop of the Year' award, but he was certainly no fool. "Suppose real trouble came along?"

Ramos grimaced, shook his head, and used the bottle to top up both glasses.

"Senhora da Costa is a pleasant woman," he said absently. "A handsome woman for her age — would you agree?"

Laird nodded. "And efficient."

"Exactly." Ramos looked pleased. "She is a widow. Her husband was an army man, killed in the Angolan fighting — she and her son were out there too. Afterwards, she came to Porto Esco, took over this place, and built it up into a good business."

"I met her son," said Laird. "He

seems to be doing all right."

"With his Companhia Tecnico?" He gave a slight frown. "The old owners got out after the revolution, when the workers' movement was trying to take over — then that faded back. Instead, José and a friend called Charles Bonner moved in. Bonner has the money and the brains, José" — he stopped and shrugged — "well, he runs the day-to-day side and plays with his boat."

"What's Bonner's background?" asked Laird. The name certainly didn't sound local.

"He knew José in Angola — he's Anglo-Portuguese."

"Like Kati Gunn?"

"*Sim.* But not so pretty." Ramos laughed at his own joke, finished his drink in a gulp, and pushed back his chair. "I have a town to look after, Senhor Laird. *Adeus* for now."

The man left, stopping at the street door to square the cap on his head, then ambling out with baton and gun bouncing at his sides. Taking time over finishing his drink, Laird signalled the barman over, paid him, then rose. A few slyly appreciative grins came his way from the other customers as he went out, but no direct greeting.

Going back through the Pousada Pico's lobby, he went into the restaurant. It was at the rear of the building, a big, cool room with crisp white linen tablecloths, and a waiter found him a table, handed him a typewritten menu, then left. A few of the other tables were occupied, one by a small family party, the rest by people who were obviously residents like himself.

He glanced at the menu, frowned at the unfamiliar dishes listed, then gave a grin of relief as Kati Gunn appeared from the kitchen. She wore a waitress uniform of black dress and apron, dumped a couple of plates of food on another of the tables, then came over to him.

"Is there anything you don't do around here?" asked Laird.

"Mama Isabel is short-staffed tonight."

She brushed a lock of tawny hair back from her forehead. "Like I told you, I help out. How's that plug I fixed?"

"Pretty sick," said Laird. "It blew."

She sighed, then nodded at the menu. "Take the *linguado*. It's fish-sole stuffed with chopped meat and ham. Mama Isabel is heavy on the olive oil, but it's good."

"Sold," agreed Laird. "Any news yet on that diver I'm looking for?"

"Yes." She made a brief business of lighting the candle on his table with a match, and he caught the tantalising scent of her perfume. "Jorges Soller got back with the *Juhno* about half an hour ago. He sent word he'll either be at his boat or at a garage called the Flores — its just off the main road from here, round the bay."

"I'll look for him once I've eaten," said Laird. "What kind of a character is he?"

"The kind who likes working on his own. But he's friendly enough, not like some of the people you've met."

Her eyes twinkled. "Mama Isabel was worried about you — that's why she sent Sergeant Ramos through to the bar. What she says, Ramos does — I think he has plans in her direction. Like he isn't interested in just ending up on a police pension."

She went off. A little later, it was the waiter who served his meal and the *linguado* was all he'd been promised and more. Laird washed it down with a light local beer, waved aside the offer of dessert, and saw Kati Gunn still serving at some of the other tables as he left.

Outside the Pico the night was cool, with a slight breeze coming in across the moonlit water of the bay. Loud, gay music was coming from a bar further along the street as he crossed over and walked slowly down the line of moored boats. A few were newly in, a few, including the rakish *Mama Isabel*, had gone. He found the *Juhno* moored beside a small, badly cracked concrete slipway where the waves rippled in and some gulls were resting.

She was a small, elderly, down-at-the-heels fishing boat with a stink of diesel oil around her and the black shape of a scuba-diving suit draped like a deflated body over a line which ran from a rickety wheelhouse to the stub of mast she carried forward. But the boat lay empty and deserted and Laird turned away.

He walked on, enjoying the night and the exercise, while the shore road followed the curve of the bay and an occasional car went past. He gave up counting the moored boats, saw only a few other people out and about, and was beginning to wonder if he'd come the wrong way when he saw a neon sign which said 'Garagem Flores' on ahead.

An arrow on the sign pointed up a side street. A stone's throw up, he reached a small filling station. It was closed, but a light showed at an open side door, a motorcycle with a sidecar luggage frame was parked outside, and as he got nearer he heard the steady throb of a compressor engine.

He went in and found the garage workshop. The compressor was over at the far side, behind a stripped-down truck, and a small, muscular man in khaki shirt and slacks was leaning beside it, watching the gauges while a scuba-diving air cylinder was recharged.

The man saw him, flicked a switch, and the compressor grunted to a halt.

"Jorges Soller?" asked Laird.

"Sim." The diver had sharp, almost Arab features, thinning dark hair and powerful stubby hands. He gave Laird a frown. "You wanted to see me, senhor . . . why?"

"Because I've read a copy of the diving survey you did on the *Craig Michael*'s hull." Laird offered Soller a cigarette, took one himself, and they shared a light.

"What about my survey, senhor?" Soller took a long draw on his cigarette, his frown deepening a little. "I said the ship's hull was intact, and it is.

64

I worked almost a whole damn day making sure. She was lucky — as lucky as any ship I've ever seen."

"You've seen a few?" asked Laird.

"I did twelve years as a diver in the Portuguese navy, an' that's experience enough for me," said the man.

"For most people," agreed Laird. "Tell me something. When you were checking the hull, why didn't you say anything in your report about how she'd refloat?"

"The marine surveyor who came down from Lisbon seemed to have his own ideas," said Soller. "I was paid to report on the hull — and I know insurance companies like yours, senhor. They say what they want, they don't pay for extras." He paused, running a stubby hand over the dull metal of the compressor casing. "Though now I hear another diver is being brought in."

"Not by my company." Laird paused. "The present plan is to let her refloat on her own with the next spring tide.

Any problems there?"

"None." Soller shook his head emphatically.

"Suppose it was tried earlier?" asked Laird.

"Earlier?" The man leaned back against the compressor and shrugged. "It might be done, but why?"

"The way she's lying, what would the risks be?" persisted Laird.

"I would have to think," said Soller. "I — yes, I would want to take another look." He considered Laird carefully. "That would take time."

"You'll be paid." Laird wondered briefly what Osgood Morris and the Clanmore accounts office would say when they found out. "When can you do it?"

"Tomorrow — but not straight away." Soller gave a slightly apologetic grin. "*Desculpe-me*. I have a busy time ahead."

"This matters," said Laird.

"*Sim.*" The diver wasn't impressed. He pointed at the air cylinders, each with a double white band painted round one end of their grey lengths. "Tonight, once I have these recharged, there is a senhora in the town who would be heartbroken if I didn't turn up."

"Lucky you," said Laird. "Where's her husband?"

"Out fishing, to pay the mortgage. Then I want a few hours sleep, and after that I have a little job of my own to do in the bay — one that matters to me." He stopped there and eyed Laird for a moment. "Senhor, let me ask you one thing. Did any other interest, apart from the tanker, bring you here?"

"None," said Laird, puzzled. "Why?"

"I was curious, that's all." Soller shrugged. "Suppose this new diver is at work when I get to the tanker?"

"You can hold hands underwater with him for all I care," said Laird. "Just get the job done."

Soller grinned, turned away, and switched the compressor on again.

Once outside the garage, Laird tossed his half-smoked cigarette away and started the return walk to the Pousada Pico with the feeling that, whatever was happening, he'd at least done something positive.

It was a good night, a peaceful night. He walked along by the sea wall, the creak of mooring ropes from the boats lined beyond it blending with the faint sound of music coming from one of the bars further along. The tune was catchy, he found himself humming to it, then the new sound of a vehicle engine made him glance back.

An old truck was trundling in his direction, moving at a sedate pace. Ignoring it, Laird kept on walking and reached a stretch where the sea wall rose to more than head height and gave shelter to a miscellany of drying nets and piled fish boxes.

Suddenly, he was pinned in a blaze of light as the truck's head lamps blazed to full beam. At the same instant its engine note changed to a high revving bellow — and he swung round in time to see the truck coming straight towards him, accelerating hard.

Trapped by the sea wall on one side, Laird broke into a desperate zigzag run while the snarl of the truck came closer and closer, the head lamps still pinning him, its driver following every move he made. When he glanced back, the radiator grille seemed almost on top of him.

A moment later Laird tripped on an old net and went sprawling. As he hit the concrete, he made a last, despairing bid to roll clear — but knew with a dull certainty it was useless.

But the inevitable didn't happen. With a squeal of tyres the truck swung away, knocking down a pile of fish boxes. They were still clattering down as the truck went into a skidding turn and disappeared up a side street.

Dazedly, Laird got used to the fact

he was still alive. He started to haul himself to his feet, dishevelled, his right knee numb with pain, then a fresh pair of head lamps caught him in their beam. A station wagon braked hard to a halt beside him and the two men aboard jumped out.

"You, Senhor Laird!" The leading figure who came hurrying over stopped short and swore in surprise. It was José da Costa, and as he helped Laird to stand up he asked quickly, "Are you all right?"

"Mendable," said Laird.

Giving a grunt of relief, da Costa beckoned his companion nearer.

"We saw what happened, just as we came along," he said, still half-supporting Laird, his dark face a study in anxiety. "That truck — some damn fool driver with too many *litros* of wine in his belly."

"What do you think, José?" asked the other man, thickset, middle-aged, and in a dark business suit. He had a clipped, flat voice that might have come straight off a South African veldt and as he spoke he scowled in the direction the truck had gone. "Do we try after him?"

"Now? It would be a waste of time," said da Costa. "Unless — " He turned to Laird. "Would you know the truck again?"

"No chance," said Laird. "It was just four wheels, an engine, and a damned great pair of head lamps."

"It might have killed you," frowned da Costa. He paused and gestured at his companion. "This is my partner, Charles Bonner — "

"And I thought like José, that you were a dead man," said Bonner. "If the driver hadn't swerved — "

Laird nodded. He'd have been killed, and the Porto Esco equivalent of a street cleaning squad would have been hosing most of him off the concrete in the morning.

"You could report it to the police," declared da Costa, then shrugged. "Sergeant Ramos's private army — no,

71

I don't suppose that would do much good."

Bonner nodded agreement. "The best thing we can do is give you a lift along to the Pico. We're heading that way."

Laird limped along with them to the station wagon, a cream-coloured four-wheel drive Range-Rover. It seated three up front and he got in, Bonner taking the wheel and da Costa taking the other seat on the passenger side.

"I was thinking," said da Costa slowly as the station wagon started up and got under way. "You had some trouble earlier, Senhor Laird. There were those fishermen — "

"It's possible." Laird winced as they lurched over a pothole and the jarring sent a fresh throb of pain through his injured knee. "But who's going to prove it?"

"Nobody, around here." Bonner changed gear with an emphatic flick. "Maybe that drunk saw us coming and changed his mind. Maybe he was just chicken — but I know one thing, mister. You were lucky."

"Even luckier that we came along," added da Costa. "Bonner dragged me out to go round to the Companhia Tecnico — we're just on our way back from there."

"Do you work a night shift at the yard?" asked Laird. "Hell, no." Bonner chuckled at the notion. "It's hard enough to get our boys to work during the day. A problem came up, that's all." He took his eyes off the road for a moment and glanced at Laird with a cool deliberation. "But we might have an even bigger problem ahead — José says he mentioned it to you."

"The loading date for your next shipment out." Laird nodded. "Let's wait and see. If there's trouble, we might talk compensation."

"You'd better." Bonner said it amiably. "I know a good lawyer." Then he chuckled again. "You know, it doesn't seem as if Porto Esco has handed you much of a welcome so far."

"Let's hope it gets better," said Laird.

A few moments later the Range-Rover stopped at the Pico, on the sea-wall side of the road. Da Costa climbed out and made an apologetic noise as Laird got out after him.

"I'll say *boa noite* because Bonner and I still have some talking to do," he explained. "But if anything more happens, or if I can help — "

"I'll let you know," said Laird. "Thanks again."

He watched the man get back into the station wagon. Then as it drove off, the taillights fading into the night, he limped a few paces to the sea wall and sat on the low concrete edging, rubbing his knee again.

His mouth a tight, thoughtful line, he looked out at the way the twinkling curve of the lights of Porto Esco reflected on the sea, then at the other, occasional pinpricks of light that showed on the land across the bay. Whether the man behind the wheel

74

of the truck had meant to kill him or just scare him might be debateable, but the difference had been a narrow margin — too narrow for comfort.

Hearing footsteps, he glanced round. The Pico's street door lay open and Kati Gunn was crossing towards him.

"I saw the way you got out of Bonner's car," she said, concern in her voice as she looked down at him. "What happened to you?"

"I side-stepped a drunken truck driver," he told her. "Bonner and José gave me a lift back. I took a tumble, that's all." He saw she was out of her waitress uniform and back in jeans and a sweater. "Don't tell me Mama Isabel ran out of things for you to do?"

"She goes early to bed." Kati sat on the parapet beside him, still frowning slightly. "The way you were limping — "

"It's a good way of getting sympathy." He gave her a mock scowl. "How hard will you be working tomorrow?"

75

"I said I'd help with the breakfasts, that's all." She raised a quizzical eyebrow. "Why?"

"Because with luck I'm going to take the afternoon off." Laird eyed her hopefully. "Like to come along?"

She smiled and nodded, then drew her feet up so she could clasp her hands around her knees.

"There's a message from the *Craig Michael* for you at the reception desk," she said. "That old engineer they've got and Jody Cruft, the bo'sun, brought it in. Then they went off on a pub-crawl — they said Captain Amos wasn't expecting an answer." She paused. "Oh, and I fixed that plug in your room again — or I tried."

"Amen," said Laird. He watched her for a moment, wondering if she had the slightest idea the kind of temptation she presented in the moonlight. "When you're not down here, what do you do for a living, Kati?"

"In Lisbon?" One finger stroked a pattern on the cool concrete beside her. "I sell plane tickets at an airline counter — the kind of job where you keep a happy smile and use plenty of deodorant. But the pay is good and I was lucky to get it."

"You weren't in Angola?"

She shook her head. "Not at the finish, not like Mama Isabel and José. My parents had the sense to pull out a couple of years before that, and they live up near Oporto now. When Mama Isabel came out, it was on the refugee airlift and she brought one small suitcase. José didn't make it until weeks later."

"How about his friend Bonner?" asked Laird.

"They met out there. Bonner was on some kind of engineering contract job — that's about all I know." She wrinkled her nose with a touch of amusement. "It was Bonner's money that bought the Companhia Tecnico. They stuck so close together after that, some people thought they were bent — till a girl in the village had to be shipped out quickly and her father left José looking like he'd collided with a wall."

Somewhere in the little town a church clock began striking, the sound carrying softly in the night air. As it finished, Kati Gunn got to her feet.

"Eleven *horas* — I'm heading for bed," she said. For a moment, her hand rested on his shoulder. "*Adeus*, Andrew — make it about three tomorrow afternoon and I'll be ready."

Laird watched the supple, long-legged way she crossed the street and went into the Pico. Then, as the door swung shut he drew a deep, appreciative breath before be turned and looked out at the bay again.

A small fishing boat was coming in from the channel, rounding the point of land which hid the stranded *Craig Michael* from sight. He thought for a moment of Captain Amos and his wife out there, two near-castaways on a monthly pay cheque, then switched his attention to the fishing boat as she drew nearer.

She passed by, engine a ragged, puttering beat, the big kerosene fishing lamp at the stern still burning brightly and a couple of fishermen moving in the fringe of the glare as they sorted out the night's catch. A soft, phosphorescent wash showed at her stern as she beaded in towards a mooring further along the bay.

Laird reached for his cigarettes, then put them away again, unused. Staying where he was, he felt the tranquility of the night soak into him, while the sound of the fishing boat gradually faded.

Tiny, twinkling lights showed here and there on the dark curve of land across the water. A few showed on the bay itself and two of them, close together, brighter than the rest, he identified as marking the approach to the Companhia Tecnico yard.

Then he narrowed his eyes and looked again, beyond the markers.

He hadn't been mistaken. There were other lights showing behind them, tiny, moving pinpricks in the night which might have been vehicle head lamps or a boat of some kind. Then, so soft and low it was almost lost in the breeze, he thought he heard the murmur of an engine.

A moment later the pinpricks of light had gone and the murmur had stopped. He puzzled over it for a moment, then shrugged. Maybe Bonner and da Costa had driven back to the yard again. It was none of his business.

He rose, limped his way across and into the Pico, crossed the deserted lobby where only a single lamp was burning, and found an envelope with his name on it lying on the desk. From there, climbing the stairs to his room was a laborious business which left him cursing. But once he arrived he found the bed had been turned down and the curtains drawn.

Throwing his jacket over a chair, he opened the envelope. The note inside was on a single sheet of paper, and Captain Amos hadn't wasted words.

"Owners advise by radio that salvage expert arrives tomorrow. Ordered give him full co-operation. Can you be around?"

Laird sighed, crumpled the note, and tossed it in the wastebasket.

Getting out of his clothes, he washed, bathed his injured knee, then padded across the room and grinned down at the new plug on the bed light flex. This time, it was already in its socket. He pressed the light switch experimentally — and the plug banged out from the wall with a flash of blue.

Still, it was a step forward. He switched out the main light, made his way across the darkened room, and collapsed thankfully on the bed.

After all, he decided, in the moments before he fell asleep, a girl like Kati Gunn didn't have to be good at everything.

★ ★ ★

81

Captain Harry Novak, tug master and self-proclaimed salvage expert, arrived in Porto Esco early the next morning aboard a rented VW minibus with a rented Portuguese driver at the wheel and two scuba divers, plus their equipment, crammed into the rear section.

It was a bright, clear day with a faint high veining of white cirrus clouds the only break in the blue sky. Leaning in the shade of the street doorway, Andrew Laird watched unemotionally as the VW stopped outside the Pousada Pico and its occupants climbed out. Novak had telephoned him from Faro airport an hour earlier, a curt call to say he'd flown in from Lisbon and was coming on by road.

The call, on its own, had been enough to tell Laird that Novak hadn't changed. Now, as Novak stood for a moment beside the VW, it was abundantly clear Laird had been right. A broad-shouldered, thick-waisted man in his mid-forties with dark, shaggy hair, he had a heavy, ill-tempered face on which a scar, running from cheekbone to eyebrow, almost obliterating it, seemed natural. Wearing an open-necked white shirt, a crumpled blue gaberdine jerkin and matching slacks, Novak looked exactly what he was — a tough, bullying individual, but still a very competent tug master.

Novak saw Laird, nodded, then turned to his men as they followed him out of the vehicle.

"Take five minutes and get yourself a beer," he told them in a loud, snarling voice. "But stay close." Then he walked straight over to Laird and looked him up and down. "So you became the boy wonder of the insurance game. Big deal."

"It's good to see you too, Captain," said Laird, still leaning against the doorway.

His eyes were on Novak's scar, the slight smile on his lips was one of memory. A sailmaker's needle and ordinary sewing cotton weren't the best of surgical tools, but it hadn't been Laird's fault that they were the only things available. Not that it had worried him.

"Flea-pit fishing villages — they're all the damned same," grunted Novak, hesitating slightly under Laird's appraisal. "All right, let's walk and talk for a minute."

"Fine," agreed Laird. "Both come free."

They set off. Further down the street the morning's fish market was under way at a line of tiny stalls newly set up along the sea wall. They passed the noisy bargaining going on around piled boxes of cod and plastic buckets filled with small squid, the air heavy with the stink of fish. Beyond that, the catch on display became exclusively sardines — small mountains of the tiny fish, being shovelled into plastic bags as fast as they were sold.

Novak halted as they reached a quieter stretch where some horse-drawn carts were waiting.

"All right, let's agree on this much," he said curtly. "You're here to do a job and I'm here to do a job. But we don't get along, we're not on the same team, and I don't give a damn."

"Understood." Laird nodded. "My job is to keep an eye on the claim situation around the *Craig Michael*. Her owners let my company know you're coming in on the act. I hear you're bringing a diver — and you arrive with two." He eyed Novak. "What's your angle?"

"Mine? Mister, let's leave that till my boys have seen the underside of that tub out there. But get this straight. I don't have to give a damn what you or your bosses think. My judgement, that's all that counts." "Then let's hope you get it right," murmured Laird.

"I will. In fact, you can come along and be right where it's happening. Be my guest."

"I'll do that," said Laird, and followed him back towards the waiting VW.

3

IT took the VW minibus ten minutes to drive the dusty, narrow road round the bay to the Companhia Tecnico yard and once clear of Porto Esco the scenery was a mixture of red, rocky soil, green cactus, and an occasional patch of wild mimosa bloom.

But that all ended as they lurched and bounced through the gate in the high wire fence which surrounded the shipbreaking yard. It was a drab sprawl of huts and slipways, separated by dumps of rusting steel plate and dismantled machinery. An old ferryboat was being reduced to scrap on the main slipway, a squad of men crawling over it armed with cutting torches. A trawler lay at the next berth, her deck works already removed, waiting her turn for oblivion.

Braking, their driver brought the minibus to a shuddering halt outside a brick-built office block. At the same moment José da Costa emerged from the building, beaming.

"Is that our boy?" asked Novak, levering himself out of his seat in the minibus.

"That's da Costa," said Laird, then grinned as another figure emerged from the building. "You're getting the full treatment — there's Bonner, his partner."

"It's costing enough." Novak swung open the minibus door and was first out.

By the time Laird had given the two scuba divers a hand with their gear the introductions were over and Novak seemed to have relaxed a little.

"*Bom dia*, Senhor Laird," said da Costa, taking a couple of steps towards him. "Captain Novak says you are coming out with us."

"If you've room to spare," said Laird.

"No problem," said da Costa, then gave him a sidelong glance. "But — ah — how do you feel? After last night, I mean."

"Like I'd love to lay my hands on a certain truck driver, that's all." Laird meant it. His knee was still stiff, but not painful. "Is Bonner coming along with us?"

"Not me." Bonner, just turning away while Harry Novak went back to his divers, had overheard. "One of us always has to be around the yard. And" — his mouth tightened slightly — "that's usually me."

"Because he has the business brain," said da Costa easily. He looked past them to Novak. "Ready, Captain?"

Novak nodded and, while Bonner went back into the office, da Costa led the little procession of men across the yard to a jetty. The *Mama Isabel* was tied up there, but da Costa went past her low, sleek hull to a small, elderly, blunt-bowed tugboat which had a wisp of steam rising from its stubby funnel.

"This?" Novak asked, startled.

"She is small," admitted da Costa. "A minnow beside your deep-sea salvage tugs, Captain. But she is reliable, and a good diving boat."

They got aboard. Two waiting deck hands helped Novak's divers with their gear while Laird and Novak were shepherded into the little open bridge by da Costa, who took the helm. A few shouted orders and, as the mooring ropes were cast off and the little tug's engine began tumbling, they eased away from the jetty and swung out into the bay.

Curious, Laird looked around as they began to leave the yard behind. Despite the shingle bank that formed the shore some distance across to their left, they were obviously in a wide deep water channel.

"A good location, eh?" said da Costa, as if reading his mind. Spinning the little steering wheel, he brought the tug butting round on a new course. "Around here, we have close on thirty fathoms under us." He shrugged. "When the yard was opened, the first owners had big plans — too big for a place like Porto Esco. Bonner and I are different. For us, small is beautiful and makes enough money."

"With what I'm paying for this hire, I'll believe you," growled Novak. Then he lit a cigarette, let it dangle from his lips, and lapsed into silence.

★ ★ ★

Nothing had changed when they reached the helpless black bulk of the *Craig Michael*. As the tug came in under the shadow of the vast hull, Harry Novak went aft and spoke briefly to his two divers, who were already pulling on their scuba gear. Then, as the tug drifted in the last few feet, her car tyre fenders bumping the tanker's side at an accommodation ladder, he returned.

"They know what to do," he told Laird. "So does da Costa. Let's go."

Laird followed him up the ladder,

while the tug immediately began manoeuvering away, towards the *Craig Michael*'s stern. Stepping onto the tanker's deck, they found a reception committee waiting. Captain John Amos was flanked on one side by his wife and on the other by Andy Dawson. The thin, elderly engineer glared suspiciously during the introductions while Jody Craft and Cheung, the rest of the *Craig Michael*'s complement, hovered not far off along the deck.

"My owners radioed you were coming, Captain Novak," said Amos. "But I still don't know exactly why you're here."

"You'll find out," Novak said. "They told you to give me full co-operation?"

Amos nodded, frowning.

"Good." Novak switched his gaze to Mary Amos. "It happens I ate breakfast on a plane and it seems a long time ago. For a start, I could use some coffee."

"I'll get it," said Mary Amos.

"Afterwards, I want a guided tour."

Novak turned back to Captain Amos as he spoke, then thumbed towards Dawson. "I'll want him along with us. But I don't need him right now."

Amos glanced at Dawson, who scowled and went off muttering. There was total silence for a moment, then Amos moistened his lips.

"Have I got clearance to do this from the insurance side?" he asked in a worried voice.

"I'm not objecting," Laird told him.

"Wouldn't matter a damn if you did," said Novak. "Mrs. Amos, how about that coffee?"

The woman flushed, rubbed a hand nervously down the front of her shirt, and led the way.

It was an anything but comfortable coffee break. Amos and his wife sat stiffly upright in the same day-cabin as before, Laird tried to stay in the background, and Harry Novak sprawled in a chair talking loudly about some of the salvage jobs he'd tackled. He sounded as if he were boasting, but

Laird knew that most of his stories were true.

"That's enough," said Novak at last, shoving his cup aside and levering his bulky body out of the chair. "Captain, I don't want to know what this ship is like topsides. I'm interested in your hull structure, your ballast tanks, and your pump layout in that order. If you collect your engineer, I'll check how my boys are getting on — then we'll start."

They left Mary Amos and went out on deck. Da Costa's tug was now lying off the *Craig Michael*'s mid-section and a thin trail of bubbles coming to the surface on the light swell showed where at least one of the divers was working. Novak stayed by the rail, watching, until Amos arrived with Andy Dawson. Then he came aggressively to life again.

"Unless I ask differently, I want facts, not opinions," he said. "If you want to come along, Laird, fine. But keep your mouth shut."

They climbed down the first of a series of long ladders that led into the dark depths of the tanker's hull. It was the start of nearly two hours of painstaking inspection, walking and crawling, up and down ladders, through innumerable hatches. Long before it was ended both Captain Amos and Dawson showed signs that their patience had been strained to the limit by the stream of questions from Novak, his insistence on answers, and his surly deliberation over layout plans.

But, reduced to a spectator's role, following and listening, Andrew Laird still had to admit that Novak was thorough — and when they at last emerged back into daylight on the main deck, the man was grinning. The grin became even wider when he saw that da Costa's tug was lying beside the ladder again.

"I'll be back," he said, and climbed down the ladder to the tug. From the deck above, Laird and Amos saw him talking earnestly to the two divers, who were back aboard and out of their scuba gear. The conversation went on, first one man then the other breaking off occasionally to sketch something on what looked like a chart they had spread over one of the tug's deck hatches.

Captain John Amos gave a long sigh. "What's it all about?" he asked.

Laird shrugged. He had a good idea, but there was no sense in anticipating.

Novak soon came back aboard and joined them. Hands in his pockets, he stopped in front of Amos.

"Captain, I'm going to put you back in business," he said. "And I don't mean when the spring tide comes along. My way, it'll be in two, maybe three days — that's why your owners hired me."

"What's the rush?" asked Laird, while Amos stared open-mouthed.

"A panic charter job, long term — and they need this ship yesterday." Harry Novak's eyes glittered. "And

95

before you say anything, they're prepared to accept all risks in refloating as long as I say it can be done."

"Have they told Clanmore Alliance any of this yet?" asked Laird.

"Its being done." Novak deliberately faced away from him, towards Amos, who still looked dazed. "Your owners will radio all the confirmation you need. They want you out of this backwater, fast."

"Fine." Amos licked his lips. "But — well, suppose something goes wrong?"

"It won't," said Novak. "But if you're unhappy, I reckon your owners could fly in someone else to take your place."

Amos flushed and for a moment his fists clenched at his sides. Then, very slowly, he nodded.

"How do I help?" he asked quietly.

"Mostly, you keep the hell out of the way," said Novak. "Three of the best and biggest salvage tugs this side of the Atlantic coast will be here by tomorrow. We'll start by blasting away a few underwater rocks that might prove awkward, then we'll play around with your ballast tanks to give the hull the kind of trim we'll need. The rest of it is routine — hauling this tub off will be as simple as pulling a cork from a bottle."

"Ignoring one little problem," said Laird. He pointed towards the stern, and the narrow gap between the *Craig Michael*'s bulk and the far side of the channel. "You'll only be able to use your tugs from the seaward side — nothing their size can squeeze into the bay."

"The answer to that is the kind of thing I get paid for," snapped Novak, but something in his manner made Laird guess he had touched a nerve ending of doubt. The tug master recovered quickly, glanced at his wristwatch, and said, "I've got to get back ashore. Ready?"

Laird nodded, but Captain Amos said, "There's a detail about insurance, from the grounding. It'll only take a moment."

Novak wasn't deceived, and showed it.

"Make it a moment," he said, and crossed to the accommodation ladder.

Amos waited until the man was on his way down to the tug, then turned to Laird.

"I had to agree," he said unhappily. "But — well, what do you think?"

"I think either your bosses have gone crazy or they're desperate," said Laird.

Chewing his lip, his dark face worried, Amos nodded. "What about Novak? Is he — "

"Capable?" Laird grimaced. "Yes. He's capable."

Any salvage job had a gambling element in it. This one, he reckoned, had the odds stacked against it — for anyone but Novak. The Anglo-Greek directorship of the Antarah Lines had to know that already. That they were still prepared to plunge on, without insurance cover, meant the chips were really down as far as they were concerned.

"God," said John Amos.

"Amen," agreed Laird. "I'll be in touch."

He left the man and made his way down to the tug. As soon as he had stepped from the ladder onto her wooden deck, the elderly engine under his feet began to rumble and they edged away from the tanker in a gathering white wash, swinging back round towards Porto Esco.

"Senhor Laird — " Da Costa's hail from the open bridge and a beckoning wave brought him over to join the man. Harry Novak was there too, leaning back against the rail, apparently absorbed in cleaning his nails with the blade of a long, thin, bone-handled clasp knife.

"Good news, eh?" said da Costa, cheerfully. "For the fishermen, for people like me — and I have told Captain Novak that the full facilities of Companhia Tecnico are at his disposal."

"At jacked-up rates," said Novak.

His eyes were hooded as he glanced at Laird. "Well, did Amos weep on your shoulder?"

Laird shrugged and said nothing. His silence seemed to anger Novak.

"Think I can't do it?" he demanded.

"Salvage isn't my game," said Laird. "You said three tugs would be here by tomorrow."

Novak nodded. "You know two of them — *Scomber* and *Beroe*. The other one is the *Santo Andre*. They've 12,000 horsepower each, enough to pull this whole damned bay out to sea."

Laird was impressed. *Scomber* was the salvage tug he'd sailed on under Novak and always worked in team with *Beroe*. The *Santo Andre* he'd only heard of, but it amounted to an impressive little flotilla. Then a sudden suspicion crossed his mind.

"Where are they coming from?" he asked.

"Lisbon." Novak smiled slightly and ran a finger down the scar on his cheek. "They sailed from the Tagus this morning."

Da Costa was smiling too, as if he'd already been let into the secret. Laird swore softly. It meant the decision to float the *Craig Michael* had been finalised even before Novak arrived with his divers.

"That's how it is, insurance man," taunted Novak. He turned to da Costa. "We'll drop him off first, on the town side of the bay. That way, he can get to a telephone quicker."

* * *

Minutes later, the little tug nudged briefly against a wooden jetty near the centre of Porto Esco, hesitated just long enough for Laird to step ashore, then thrashed away again, steering for the shipbreaking yard side of the bay.

Leaving the jetty, walking along the street towards the Pousada Pico, Laird gave a tight-lipped frown as he glanced at his watch. It was coming up to noon, a good time to catch Osgood Morris at his desk in the Clanmore office in London. But he had another matter on his mind. Jorges Soller had promised he'd be out and diving at the *Craig Michael* as soon as he could. Yet his *Juhno* was still lying in the line of craft moored to the sea wall.

Lengthening his stride, he went past the Pico and reached the old diving boat. The cabin door was lying open, but no one answered when he hailed, so he stepped aboard.

His footsteps on the deck brought a movement in the cabin doorway. Then, to Laird's surprise, it was Sergeant Ramos who stepped out. His face more like a block of wood than ever, the policeman studied him impassively.

"Where's Jorges Soller?" asked Laird.

"Not here, Senhor Laird." Sergeant Ramos's lips twisted slightly. "Was he expecting you?"

"The other way round. He's supposed to be out doing a job for me." Laird had a sudden sense of foreboding.

"Something happened to him?"

"Sim." Ramos gave a slow, irritating nod. "Come inside, senhor. You will have to find yourself another diver."

Ducking his head, Laird followed the man into the *Juhno*'s cabin. It was small and cramped, with a stale smell compounded of damp, sweat, and old cooking odours. Grubby bedding lay crumpled on a bunk, topped by discarded clothing. An opened locker was filled with patched diving gear and a collection of empty wine bottles, while the small table in the middle of the cabin was covered by a scatter of papers.

"Soller is dead," said Ramos. He paused as a cockroach scurried for cover across the cabin deck, then one large foot stepped on it. "His body was washed up on the beach this morning — soon after you left, Senhor Laird."

"Dead?" Laird needed a moment to take in the news. "How?"

"A diving accident, or so it seems." Sergeant Ramos switched to a careful formality. "He was wearing full scuba-diving equipment — the cause of death is still a puzzle, but there is an autopsy being carried out now." He paused. "I was told you talked to him last night."

Laird nodded. "At the Flores garage. I asked him to carry out another survey dive at the *Craig Michael*."

"And he agreed?"

"Yes."

The wooden face wrinkled in a slight frown. "Did he say anything else?"

"Something about a date with a woman, and that he had another diving job scheduled before he could tackle mine," said Laud.

"Obrigado." Sergeant Ramos poked at the papers on the table. "I have been looking through his things. Soller seems to have made more money from his diving than any of us guessed."

"Maybe he was just careful," said Laird dryly, glancing round the shabby little cabin.

"Perhaps." Ramos sucked his teeth

doubtfully. "Senhor Laird, I would like you to come with me — a little trip to the mortuary. We can use your car."

Laird raised an eyebrow, but nodded. Carefully closing the cabin door behind him as they left, Ramos led the way through the mid-day heat to the Pousada Pico. The few customers at the pavement tables outside watched with interest as they went round into the cool shade of the courtyard. Reaching the yellow Simca, grimacing at its fly-specked windows, Laird went to unlock the doors, then heard Sergeant Ramos give a sudden, interested grunt. Isabel da Costa was coming towards them from the *pousada*'s side door.

"Senhora" — the policeman's voice became a pleased purr — "as you see, I found him. But thank you for helping."

"Sergeant." For a moment, Mama Isabel's fine-boned face looked younger and almost coy under Ramos's gaze, then she gave a quick, professional smile at Laird. "Sergeant Ramos came looking for you earlier, Senhor Laird. But there have also been telephone calls, from London — "

"From a man called Morris?" asked Laird resignedly.

She nodded, one hand slightly adjusting the neck of her blouse while her eyes strayed back to Ramos.

"He seemed anxious to speak to you," she said. "So far, he has called three times — I took one call, Kati spoke to him the other times."

"I've got to go with the sergeant," said Laird. "But if he tries again, tell him I'll be in touch."

He opened the Simca, waited until a plainly reluctant Sergeant Ramos got into the passenger seat, then grinned at the woman, slid behind the wheel, and set the little car moving. Ramos gave a sigh as they drove out of the courtyard, then lit one of his slim, strong-smelling cheroots and began giving him directions.

★ ★ ★

Porto Esco's *posto da policia* was a small, shoe box-shaped building at the rear of the town, a place with thick white walls, narrow window slits, and the kind of door which looked as though it would have withstood a battering ram. They parked outside, in the space between an elderly Mercedes police car and a smart, glinting Volvo station wagon.

"Our *médico*," said Sergeant Ramos with a touch of envy, pointing towards the Volvo. "He should be done by now."

It was cool and quiet inside the police station. A solitary constable, tunic unfastened and pecking one-fingered fashion at a typewriter keyboard, was the only occupant in the front office. Ramos nodded at the man, beckoned Laird to follow, and led the way through the back. They passed a row of empty cells, went down a short corridor, and Ramos opened a door.

They had reached the mortuary. It was a large brick room without windows but brightly lit and with two steel autopsy tables in the middle. One of the autopsy tables had a sheet drawn over what was lying on it and the concrete floor was still damp, as if it had been hosed down. There were drainage gutters round the edges of the room.

"Wait here, *por favor*," said Ramos, and walked across to a small, partitioned area to the right. He opened another door and went in. Laird caught a glimpse of a thin, elderly man sitting in his shirt sleeves at a desk, writing, a glass of wine beside him and what looked like an opened picnic basket close at hand, then the door closed again.

A low murmur of conversation reaching his ears, he looked around again. A set of diving rubbers and scuba gear, including air tanks, was carefully arranged on a bench to one side. The tanks had white double-line paint markings like the ones he'd seen Soller with the night before.

After another moment the door

opened again and Sergeant Ramos came out, accompanied by the other man.

"Our *médico*, Dr. Gomez," said Ramos. He let Gomez murmur a greeting, then went straight on. "Senhor Laird, when you met Soller at the garage last night, what was he doing?"

"Recharging his air cylinders," said Laird.

"These?" Sergeant Ramos pointed at the twin cylinders on the bench.

"They've got the same markings," said Laird.

"And he was using the garage compressor?" asked Ramos.

Laird nodded and saw the two men exchange a glance. Sergeant Ramos looked almost bewildered, Dr. Gomez had the makings of a satisfied smile on his lips.

"So what killed him?" asked Laird.

"The air in these tanks," said Sergeant Ramos. He turned to the *médico* for help.

"Carbon monoxide," said Dr. Gomez

in a dry, factual voice. "It showed in the blood tests I ran, but even before that — " He led the way over to the shape on the autopsy table, lifted a corner of the sheet, and let them look for a moment.

In death, Jorges Soller's face had a relaxed expression. But his complexion was almost cherry-red in colour.

"Sometimes it happens." Dr. Gomez lowered the sheet again and shrugged. "A diver is careless, or there is a leak he does not know about in the exhaust pipe from the compressor engine. Then fumes from the engine are sucked into the compressor itself and from there into his air tanks — waiting to kill him."

"You mean the moment he began using these tanks — "Laird fell silent, vague memories stirring in his mind from medical school lectures. Carbon monoxide had no taste, no odour, no colour, and gave little warning. It insinuated its way into the blood stream, exertion quickening the process.

"He would gradually feel tired, then weak, then he would become unconscious," said Dr. Gomez.

"Oxygen starvation," said Laird softly. "Fatal saturation anywhere between 60 and 80 per cent."

"Sim." Dr. Gomez raised a slightly surprised eyebrow. "And, naturally, the effects are considerably accelerated when a man is breathing compressed air." He turned to Sergeant Ramos. "Of course, the air in these tanks will have to be properly analysed."

Ramos nodded gloomily. "We'll check the compressor at the garage. Then" — he swore under his breath at the thought — "then there will be the usual reports to be made. The damned fool should have known better."

"A glass of wine before you go, Sergeant?" suggested Dr. Gomez sympathetically. "I can even offer you and Senhor Laird a sandwich if you like. My wife always packs too big a lunch for me — "

"Here?" Ramos looked around with

unconcealed distaste and shook his head quickly. "*Adeus*, Doctor. Let me know when you've checked those cylinders."

He led Laird out of the mortuary, through to the front office again, then leaned on the counter with a sigh. The same constable was still pecking monotonously at his typewriter.

"So," he said, leaning against the counter like a tired, middle-aged bear. "All I have to do now is explain in my report what that fool Soller was doing out in the bay at 3 A.M." He took a vicious swipe at a fly that had landed beside him and missed. "That's Dr. Gomez's estimate of time of death — 3 A.M. Senhor Laird, you're sure he wasn't working for you?"

"No way." Laird shook his head emphatically. "For what I wanted, he needed all the daylight he could get, shallow-dive style."

"Then *por qué*?" Sergeant Ramos sucked his lips, seemed on the brink of saying something, then obviously changed his mind. But after a moment's silence, he said, "Whatever he was doing, we can't find his motorcycle — when we do, that might help."

"Didn't he have a sideline in shellfish?" asked Laird.

"At that hour?" Ramos snorted, then glanced at his wristwatch. "If you're going back to the Pico, I'll come with you. I want to see that damned compressor at the Flores garage."

"Don't you ever use your own car?" asked Laird politely.

"With *gasolina* the price it is?" The man looked shocked.

★ ★ ★

The staff at the Flores garage were on their lunch break, which meant they were dozing in the shade around the back of the building. But Sergeant Ramos got the workshop foreman on his feet, and, with Laird trailing them, they went in to inspect the compressor unit.

113

Whatever Ramos had said, the foreman didn't like it. He stood scowling while the burly policeman poked and prodded his way around the compressor, its diesel power unit, and finally the exhaust trunking which led to the outside air. Then Ramos turned, beckoned Laird nearer, and pointed.

"There." He indicated a narrow slit in the worn trunking. "Rust and age" — he swung on the foreman — *"partido. Tem uma fuga."*

The man reacted indignantly. Growling, Sergeant Ramos grabbed him by the shoulder and shoved his face close to the split. *"Partido."*

"Partido." The foreman licked his lips uneasily as Ramos let him go.

"That would do it," said Laird quietly. "The break is close enough to the intake. When the diesel was running — "

Sergeant Ramos nodded, talked in a low rumble to the foreman for another moment in a way that made the man look one stage short of terrified, then turned away with a shrug.

"Finished?" asked Laird.

"For now," said Ramos wearily. "I'm going back to my office — to think for a little. Then I'll take another look at Soller's boat."

"When you're finished, I'd like to see any notes he left about the *Craig Michael*," said Laird. "Any objection?"

"None." Ramos answered him almost absently. "But leave it till this evening. I have something of my own to work out, Senhor Laird, and it could take me till then."

He went away, the holstered gun and baton joggling at his hips, his stride slow and thoughtful.

Driving back to the Pousada Pico, Andrew Laird left the yellow Simca in the courtyard, walked through a deserted lobby, and went straight up to his room. He splashed some water on his face, towelled it off, lit a cigarette, then lifted the telephone and waited a full couple of minutes before the call was answered. Then, surprisingly, it was Kati Gunn's voice that came on the line.

"Sorry," she said breathlessly. "I'm just standing in for Mama Isabel — she went out for a spell."

"I'm not complaining." Laird grinned at the telephone mouthpiece. "Can you get me that London number that's been calling?"

"Yes." She hesitated. "Andrew, I've still got the afternoon free. But I know about Jorges Soller, so — "

"I answered some questions, I've got to talk to my boss in London, but after that I'm ready." Laird drew on his cigarette, struck by an idea. "Have you eaten?"

"No, but — "

"Put some sandwiches and a bottle of wine in a paper sack, give me fifteen minutes, and we'll be on our way," he said firmly. "All right?"

"Twenty minutes," she countered. "I've got to change. And hold on for your call."

He caught the Clanmore Alliance

office in London just on the lunch hour but Osgood Morris hadn't gone out. He came on the line within seconds and sounded peevish.

"Where have you been?" he demanded.

"Out at the *Craig Michael*, then at a mortuary," said Laird. "A diver I hired got himself killed."

"Working for us?"

"No, free-lancing." Laird heard Morris's sigh of relief over the crackling line and grimaced. "Osgood, how much do you know about what's going on out here?"

"We had the Antarah Lines' lawyer on the doorstep first thing this morning." Over the line, Morris's voice crackled and faded for a moment, then came through strongly. "He went straight to the chairman who — ah — called me in immediately."

"No show without Punch," agreed Laird. "So?"

"We've agreed. They'll make their own immediate attempt to refloat the tanker, with all insurance cover suspended. Any outstanding claim relating to the stranding will be dropped — which saves us a few thousand pounds, even though there's no hull damage." Morris sounded smug.

"But what the hell's going on?" asked Laird savagely. "That thug Harry Novak has three tugs arriving tomorrow, he says he'll use explosives if necessary — "

"And the Antarah Lines have a twelve-month prime rate charter for the *Craig Michael* if they can have her sailing within the next four days," said Morris with an irritating patience. "She'll go back on full cover with us the moment she's under way. Good business all round — and we're not left with the refloating risk."

Laird sighed. "Who's chartering her?"

"They haven't told us yet," admitted Morris. "Their lawyer made a noise about commercial secrecy — there are too many other people on the market with spare tonnage."

"Can't you find out?" Laird scowled

at the receiver. If nothing else, Osgood Morris had a reputation for keeping his ear to the ground.

"Let's say I've — ah — heard a whisper," said Morris. "A couple of the Antarah directors had lunch yesterday with the Russian commercial attaché in London — and when it comes to this kind of deal, the Russians pay in good, old-fashioned capitalist dollars."

"Great," said Laird bitterly. "So what do you want me to do? Come home?"

"No." Morris surprised him. "Stay at Porto Esco, do nothing, but keep an eye on things. We've still an interest to protect if we've to reinsure the hull after your friend Novak is successful."

"And suppose he ends up wrecking her across the Cabo Esco channel?" asked Laird.

"Then you leave, quickly," said Morris cheerfully. "We — ah — wouldn't want to know."

The Clanmore end of the line went dead as he hung up. Laird waited a moment before he replaced his own receiver but this time there was no eavesdropping click from the Pico switchboard. Which meant that either Kati was still down there or the da Costa family had lost interest in him.

Kati Gunn was leaning against the Simca when he went out into the courtyard a few minutes later. She looked cool and beautiful in a pastel green halter-neck dress, her tawny hair tied back by a matching ribbon, and the paper sack of picnic food he'd suggested was waiting on the car's roof.

"Where are we going?" she asked as he opened the car door and stowed the sack into the rear.

"Your choice." He slapped the car keys into her hand and slid into the front passenger seat. "Just make it somewhere peaceful where I don't need to give a damn."

She looked at him in an oddly thoughtful way for a moment, then, saying nothing, got behind the wheel and started the engine.

They drove inland at first, away from the bay, through low hills which were covered in dark green scrub pines, the hollows between a mixture of coarse grass and cactus, punctuated by an occasional strip of cultivated red soil or a crumbling, grey-white adobe shack which always seemed to have children and a dog outside it.

Kati Gunn hummed as she drove, keeping the Simca at a brisk, dust-stirring pace yet seldom needing to touch the brakes.

They were on a side road, heading roughly east. Traffic meant an occasional horse-drawn cart laden with vegetables and once or twice a woman riding sidesaddle on a donkey which had bulging pannier bags. Men and women alike wore broad-brimmed soft hats, the men in serge trousers, braces and boots, the women in black peasant dresses and the same weight of footwear. Each time, Kati waved a greeting and it was returned — once by a thin, grinning young man who was laboriously shoving himself along in a lightweight wheelchair.

"Know him?" asked Laird.

She shook her head. "Just that he's ex-Army, from the African fighting." Her eyes clouded for a moment. "It was a damned fool waste of everything — I think I hate every kind of politician ever invented."

"There are all kinds of casualties," mused Laird. "But some of them mend."

"Like Mama Isabel?" Kati's lips tightened. "I've heard her crying in the night a few times." Then she drew a deep breath and gave him a smile. "Finish — I'm not going to make it that kind of an afternoon."

The road topped a rise, and suddenly the sea was in sight again, a thin blue line ahead which gradually grew while the car travelled through land which was a flat plain of boulder-strewn yellow soil, the sparse grass studded with clumps of cactus and prickly pear.

The Simca was the only thing that moved on the road, the last of the adobe houses had been left behind. Humming again, Kati turned the car off the road, they bounced along a potholed track, and then, almost without warning, they were at the edge of the sea.

Coasting down a final slope, they stopped under the shade of a high ledge of worn sandstone rock. When they got out, Laird carrying the paper food sack, small lizards scurried from their path and insects buzzed around the thin scrub. They'd come only a few miles, yet the little crescent-shaped bay spread before them was totally empty.

"Like it?" asked Kati.

Laird nodded and took a deep breath, a light breeze from the land bringing the scent of cactus to blend with the tang of the sea air.

"I thought any place like this had a hotel dumped on it, complete with package tours," he said as they walked down to the sand.

"Cousin José showed it to me first." Her eyes twinkled. "That was when he got being related mixed up with relationships. But he learned." She pointed seaward. "That's the Gulf of Cádiz — and that's Spain on the horizon."

He nodded, reckoning they could be only a few miles from the land frontier. The Spanish coast line was just a low haze with a couple of dots which were ships sailing towards it.

They stopped at a flat outcrop of rock at the edge of the lapping waves. Laird laid down the food sack, saw Kati had already kicked off her shoes, then watched while she dabbled her feet in the water.

Suddenly, she smiled at him and slipped out of the green halter-neck. Underneath it she was wearing a simply cut brown two-piece swimsuit. She stood for a moment, a slim, beautifully tanned figure, then she turned and plunged into the sea. Another moment, and she was swimming.

Laird forgot he was hungry. Still watching the girl, he got out of his own clothes, left them lying in a heap beside the green halter-neck, then followed her in.

He caught up with her after a few strokes. She laughed, dived down, and surfaced again further out.

They played that way, like children, in the warm, clear water. Then a moment came when they surfaced together, face to face. Laird's arms went round her, their lips met in a way that held a mutual want and decision, and they turned towards the shore.

Hand in hand they left the water. The sand beside the shelf of rock was soft and warm and welcoming to their bodies, still damp from the sea; the world became a total, private urgency which shut out everything else in a way and a need that Laird had never quite experienced before.

Afterwards, they lay close together,

quietly, Kati's eyes bright as she ran a tracing finger gently over the dragon tattoo on his left arm.

"Mind if I tell you something you maybe won't like?" she said suddenly.

"Go on." He half-turned to face her.

"I'm hungry."

He grinned, kissed her, and watched while she unselfconsciously slipped the green halter-top on. Then, while she began emptying the food sack, he pulled on his shirt and slacks. He was putting on his shoes when something caught his eye on the high rise of sandstone which marked the inland edge of the beach.

It was a momentary glint, a flash. Deliberately, he stooped to adjust the shoes and simultaneously watch the spot.

The same glint showed again, then a scrub bush shivered in a way that had nothing to do with the breeze.

"Kati" — he said it softly — "just keep doing things. But I think we've got company and I'm going to find out."

She froze for a moment, then gave a slight nod and began unwrapping a package from the sack. Casually, hands in his pockets, Laird began to stroll along the sand as if heading towards where they'd left the Simca. His route brought him parallel to the sandstone rise, close in, then he suddenly sprang towards it and went scrambling up.

As he climbed, moving fast, he heard a grunt, a frantic rustle — then had to fling himself sideways, diving for cover against the rock as a shot rang out and a bullet whined off a ledge close enough to shower him with tiny splinters of stone. When he raised his head, a second shot, the quick, sharp crack of a small-calibre weapon, sent another bullet ricocheting too close for comfort and this time a stone chip stung his face.

Laird glanced back. Kati was on her feet, staring openmouthed. He waved for her to stay where she was and waited, dry-mouthed.

The seconds dragged past. Then there was a third shot, but somewhere farther away. A moment later, he heard the snarl of an engine starting up and the sound of tyre-spin on gravel.

Cursing, Laird pounded up the rest of the rise and came to a frustrated stop at the top, just in time to see a motorcycle leaving a trail of dust as it headed away from him, skidding round a bend in the track and out of sight. The rider was a mere shape hunched over the handle bars.

Taking a deep breath, Laird stooped beside the patch of scrub and picked up two shining brass cartridge cases. As he examined them, his mouth tightened. Would-be Peeping Toms didn't usually go out armed — and the cases were for long-nosed .22 rifle ammunition. Shrugging, he put the cartridge cases in his pocket, then, remembering the third shot, walked across to the Simca.

One of the front tyres was flat, a bullet hole bored neatly through the rubber sidewall. Swearing wearily this time, he turned and went back down to where Kati stood waiting.

Her face was pale, she was holding a bottle of wine in one hand like a club.

"Relax," said Laird, and grinned at her. "I'm still hungry. Let's eat."

4

IT was early evening when they arrived back in Porto Esco. Changing the Simca's tyre had been a sweated labour job, one of the hub nuts refusing to budge until Laird had practically battered it into submission.

He drove. Most of the way they talked, then argued about what had happened. Kati Gunn wanted to find Sergeant Ramos and put him to work. When Laird tried to talk her out of it, her reaction was disbelief.

"Suppose you were still lying back there, wounded?" she demanded as they topped a rise and the long hump of Cabo Esco and the blue water of the bay showed ahead.

"Then I'd want a doctor, not a cop," said Laird patiently. He played his final card. "Tell Ramos, and he'll go straight to your aunt with the story — and are you going to try to tell him we were just looking at the scenery all the time?" His eyes on the road, he chuckled. "Well, it could be interesting."

She swore at him, then gave in.

"So we just do nothing?" she asked, forcing an answering smile as a child perched on top of a plodding, overloaded donkey waved a greeting.

"We say nothing," he corrected. "If I'm right, someone was out keeping tabs on me. The Peeping Tom bit was incidental."

"And that's supposed to make everything fine?" she asked indignantly. "Anyway, why follow you around?"

Laird shrugged. "Because there's some high-powered wheeling and dealing going on over the *Craig Michael*."

"Involving you?"

"Somebody seems to think so," he said.

She sighed, stopped asking questions, and settled back in her seat as the Simca reached the first small cottages which marked the start of Porto Esco.

The town and the waterfront seemed as quiet as ever. When they arrived at the Pousada Pico, Laird drove into the courtyard at the rear, parked the car, then laid a hand on Kati's arm as she reached to open the passenger door.

"Kati, it was a pretty special afternoon," he said softly.

She put her free hand over his for a moment, gave a slow smile, and nodded.

They left the car and went from the sunlight and long shadows of the courtyard into the cool of the Pico's lobby. As they entered, two people rose from a couch in a corner.

"Mr. Laird — " Captain Amos's voice sounded hoarse. He crossed over, while his wife stood waiting. "Can I talk to you?"

Surprised, Laird glanced at Kati. She gave an understanding nod, murmured an excuse, and left them. Captain Amos moistened his lips, watching her vanish from sight down a corridor.

"Sorry," he said awkwardly. "I — hell,

I couldn't think of anyone else to come and see. That's the truth, I suppose. So Mary and I came ashore and — well, just waited."

"If you want to talk, let's do that." Laird led the *Craig Michael*'s captain back to where his wife waited. Mary Amos was wearing a shore-going cotton dress, she looked strained and worried, and suddenly Laird noticed the red weal of colour which marked one side of Captain Amos's face, near the cheekbone.

"Sit down," he suggested, dragging a chair over to face the couch. He waited until they'd settled, then raised an eyebrow. "Well?"

"Captain Novak came out to the tanker again this afternoon," said Amos. "We — " he glanced sideways at his wife — "well, I had a run-in with him."

Laird gave a soft, resigned whistle. "And who thumped who first?"

"I did, I suppose, but — "

"But if he hadn't, I'd have done

133

it," said Mary Amos. She ran a hand quickly, self-consciously, over her red hair. "Mr. Laird, maybe I should tell you."

"As long as somebody does," agreed Laird.

"They came back out this afternoon in that old tug of José da Costa's — except da Costa wasn't aboard. It was his partner, Bonner. Captain Novak came aboard, said he wanted to check some details, then started throwing his weight around."

"He's good at it," said Laird.

"Very good," she said bitterly. "He — well, Cheung, our utility man, got in his way. Novak grabbed him, threw him against one of the tank vent covers, then began cursing him."

"Mary got there first," said Amos in the same hoarse voice as before. "She told Novak to lay off, and he started cursing her. So I took a swing at him — "

"A good one?" asked Laird.

"Not good enough." Amos's hand

134

went up to his cheek, for a moment. "Novak landed this one on me, and a couple more. By then, Jody Cruft and old Dawson were both coming up at the run and" — he paused, shaking his head in disbelief — "hell, Novak pulled a gun on us. Started shouting as if he was crazy, telling us he'd use it the next time anyone got in his way."

"So?"

Amos shrugged. "So we let him go, mister. What else?"

"The man had been drinking," said Mary Amos. Her broad-boned, freckled face tightened angrily. "Mr. Laird, if John cabled our owners — "

"They want the *Craig Michael* back in business, Mrs. Amos," said Laird. "Replacing Novak would take time they haven't got." He looked at Amos again, saw the way the small, thick-set man's jacket bulged at one pocket, and sighed. "It doesn't help if your husband is damned fool enough to come ashore like this was the Normandy beaches.

135

I'll take that gun, Captain — now, if you want me to help."

Reluctantly, Amos reached into his pocket and brought out a revolver. Laird took it from him and fought down a smile. It was an old, long-barrelled Smith and Wesson .38, fully loaded, speckled with rust, and it had all the appearance of having lain in a drawer most of its life.

"Ever use this?" he asked.

"No." Amos flushed. "But I've had it a long time, and — "

"And you might hit a barn door with it if you tried hard." Laird shoved the revolver into the waistband of his slacks. "Any other bright ideas, Captain?"

"Just one." Amos glanced at his wife. "I want Mary to stay ashore over the next few days."

"He made me pack a bag," said Mary Amos resignedly. "I'd rather stay with him, but he went into one of his impossible Welsh moods. So — well, maybe I'll be one problem less."

"This time, I agree with him," said Laird. He turned to Amos again. "Where's Novak now?"

Amos shrugged. "Probably at the Companhia Tecnico yard. He left on their tug."

"I'll handle him." Laird got to his feet. "I'll get a room for your wife here, then you'd better head back to your ship."

Leaving them, he went over to the reception desk and pressed the bell. After a moment, Isabel da Costa emerged from the rear office.

"*Boa tarde*, Senhor Laird," she said, with an interested twinkle in her eyes. "Did you enjoy your outing with Kati?"

"Yes, we drove around." Laird was caught off guard for a moment, but Mama Isabel's smile stayed friendly and he decided Kati hadn't talked. "Captain Amos's wife needs a room ashore for a couple of nights. Can you cope?"

The woman hesitated, her smile fading. Then she nodded, but came closer and lowered her voice.

"Senhor Laird, I know there was trouble out on their ship this afternoon — "

"You've got a good grapevine," said Laird dryly.

"You don't understand." She shook her head. "I have a room. But I also have Captain Novak and his two men staying here tonight."

"I don't think that'll be any problem," Laird said. "At least, none your friend Sergeant Ramos couldn't handle."

Isabel da Costa raised a well-plucked eyebrow, then gave a very slight nod. She walked over to Amos and his wife, collected them, and began guiding them towards the stairway leading to the guest rooms.

Giving Amos a smile as they passed, Laird went back out into the courtyard. Climbing into the Simca again, he took the revolver from his waistband and hefted it in his hand for a moment before stowing it under the passenger seat. Then, starting the car, he drove out of the courtyard and took the road round the bay towards the shipbreaking yard.

* * *

The day was over for the Companhia Tecnico work squad and they were drifting out of the yard gate in twos and threes, some on bicycles, some walking, a few jammed into old cars. Laird steered past them at a crawl, parked outside the office block, and went straight in.

The only person in the main office was a girl in her twenties who had obviously just finished for the night and was putting the cover on her typewriter. She glanced up, surprised.

"I'm looking for Captain Novak," said Laird.

Before she could answer, a door behind her clicked open and José da Costa grinned out.

"I saw you drive up, Senhor Laird," he said, dismissing the girl with a nod. "Come on through."

139

Laird crossed over and went into the room. Heeling the door shut, da Costa let his grin fade a little and considered him cautiously.

"You want Novak?" he asked.

Laird nodded.

"He's with Bonner somewhere, in the yard." Da Costa perched on one of the two desks in the room. "They're making engineer noises at each other — we're giving him some help with the *Craig Michael*, equipment he needs."

"Like what?" Laird glanced around. Apart from the desks, the room had some filing cabinets and not much else except a large, framed photograph on one wall. It was a fuzzy blowup of what had probably been an amateur snapshot and the two men grinning at the camera were da Costa and Bonner. The background seemed to be jungle and both were carrying machine pistols.

"Angola, before things got bad," said da Costa. "It helps when the men start making labour union noises — lets them remember we've had our own hard times." He offered Laird a cigarette from a box, shrugged when it was refused, and lit one for himself. "Novak wants us to help him rig sheer legs and cables from the shore to the tanker. He's also talking about things he calls drag anchors — wanting all the old anchor chain we've got."

Laird nodded. Harry Novak was trying to solve one of the biggest problems he faced in refloating the tanker. If she came away too quickly, her stern could easily ground on the opposite side of the channel. But if he could provide what amounted to a series of progressive brakes, properly positioned, coming free could be a gradual, controlled movement. It wasn't new as ideas went — shipyards often did something similar when it came to launches into a narrow channel.

"They'll be back in a moment." Da Costa hesitated. "Senhor Laird, if it concerns the — ah — disagreement Captain Novak and Captain Amos had this afternoon — "

"It might," said Laird.

"Maybe my partner and I are a little to blame," said da Costa diplomatically. "Captain Novak had lunch with us and he had — well, a few drinks."

"You mean he got stoned," said Laird.

"Let's say he was *sede* . . . that he showed a considerable capacity." Da Costa gave an uneasy laugh. "But perhaps there was some provocation later. I wasn't with him, of course — I had work to do here, in the yard, and Bonner took him out." Still perched on the desk, he shook his head. "Yes, it has been a difficult day."

"For a few people," said Laird.

Da Costa blinked, then nodded. "For you too, of course — this sad business of Jorges Soller being killed, just when he was going to work for you. A strange accident — Sergeant Ramos told me how it happened." He paused. "What will you do now, Senhor Laird? Bring in another diver?"

"I'll think about it." Laird crossed over to the window and looked out.

The sun was setting and the dark outlines of the yard cranes were etched black against the bay, which glinted like liquid gold. He drew a deep breath, mentally cursing the Harry Novaks of the world, then his eyes narrowed. An old truck was parked near the main slipway, a truck which seemed oddly familiar.

A wild, outrageous possibility came into his mind. Then, as he heard the room door open behind him, he forgot it and swung round as Charles Bonner came in with Harry Novak just behind him.

"We've a visitor," said da Costa quickly, coming down from his perch on the desk and giving Bonner a warning glance.

Bonner stopped where he was, a slight frown on his broad face. But Harry Novak pushed forward into the middle of the room.

"What the hell do you want, Laird?"

143

he asked. "I thought I spelled it out to you — you're not needed around here any more."

"Other people think differently, Captain." Laird walked over and looked him up and down more calmly than he felt. "I was right. You haven't changed."

"You mean Amos?" A scowl twitched across Novak's scarred face. "Now wait — "

"I mean you're still a bullying louse," said Laird. He saw Novak's eyes take on a hard glitter, knew what was coming, and deliberately kept on. "Why not start something with me, Captain? Or would you need a few more drinks first?"

A rumbling growl came from deep down in Novak's throat. He started to move — and Laird didn't wait. His right fist slammed a short, pistoning blow into the pit of the man's stomach, sending Novak staggering. The tug master whooped for breath, started to come forward again, and suddenly Charles Bonner was in between them.

144

"No, Captain," he said sharply, grabbing Novak by the arm and hauling him back. "I said no." He met Novak's glare for a moment, then swung round towards Laird. "If you want to brawl, make it somewhere else — not here."

Laird shrugged. Still breathing heavily, Novak moistened his lips.

"So maybe I had a drink too many," he said hoarsely. "But nobody talks to me that way — "

Da Costa sighed from the background. "Except as you say yourself, Captain, you have an important job to do. Perhaps Senhor Laird now feels happier and if an apology is due to Captain Amos and his wife, a few words would matter little — not compared with refloating the *Craig Michael*, eh?"

Novak shook himself loose from Bonner's grip, then nodded reluctantly.

"I'll pat them on the head," he said. "Will that do?"

"If things stay that way," said Laird, his face expressionless. "Amos's wife has moved ashore. You could start with her."

Novak swore under his breath, but nodded.

"So everything is peaceful." Da Costa faced Laird again. "Would you call this a regular part of insurance cover, Senhor Laird?"

"Personal liability," said Laird. "Sometimes we throw it in as a bonus."

He started for the door, but Charles Bonner got there first.

"Tell me one thing," said Bonner in his clipped, flat voice. "What do you think the chances are for the tanker?"

"Getting her off in this rush?" Laird glanced at Novak, who met his gaze sullenly. "You're working with the only tug master in the salvage game who can maybe do it — if he doesn't end up in a cage first."

He left them before anyone could reply.

* * *

Outside, he was in the car and driving out of the Companhia Tecnico yard before he remembered the old truck. He cursed softly, but it was too late to turn back — and the notion he'd had earlier was a wild one anyway.

Except that the notion stayed with him as he drove, at the same time as his thoughts strayed back to Harry Novak. Then he smiled to himself, remembering da Costa's sardonic query about insurance cover.

It had been reckoned more than once that if you put a marine insurance lawyer to work he could find small-print reasons which gave cover for almost every eventuality — then just as many small-print reasons which could let the company concerned off the hook if it felt inclined.

The marine insurance game was a labyrinth. Even the basic hull insurance policy document ran to well over three hundred lines of small print, starting with collisions at sea and ending with a coy reference to nuclear explosions. It was a business where, in the second half of the twentieth century, the insurance cover on a single ship carrying an ordinary cargo could run into several million pounds.

Cover for what the standard international insurance policies still described as 'Adventures and Perils' of a voyage.

'Of the Seas, Men-of-war, Fire, Enemies, Pirates, Rovers, Thieves . . . of all Kings, Princes and People, of what Nation, Condition or Quality soever'. The paraphrased wisp of antiquated wordage came to his lips as he drove on.

Clanmore Alliance and its Opposition used the most advanced computer technology to calculate premiums. But none of the whole league of insurance giants would dream of abandoning the quaint, seventeenth-century phraseology of their standard contracts. Every line, every word had been tested internationally by generations of jurors and change might be dangerous.

It worked, it made money in a

sophisticated gamble on 'Adventures and Perils', which, despite their modern dress, hadn't really changed in basic terms. It still needed, above all, people prepared to back a hunch and overrule a computer print-out.

Laird chuckled. Computers weren't really programmed to back hunches, or indulge in guesswork. The Clanmore Alliance unit was probably suffering indigestion from the information fed into it about a place called Cabo Esco and a risk named the *Craig Michael*.

Though if things got too bad it could always blow a fuse . . .

* * *

Sunset was giving way to dusk again and the fishing boats moored along the Porto Esco sea wall had thinned in number. A police car was parked at the section where Jorges Soller's boat was berthed and Laird eased his foot on the accelerator and brought the Simca coasting to a halt behind it.

The police car was empty but lights showed from the *Juhno*'s cabin windows in the greying dusk. Walking over, Laird stepped aboard, heard noises coming from below, saw the cabin door lying open, and climbed down, ducking his head as he went through the low entry. Then he stopped, surprised. The cabin, an untidy shambles before, now looked as though it had been hit by a miniature whirlwind. Lockers had been emptied, bedding dumped, an inspection hatch in the deck planking had been opened up — and in the middle of the chaos, tunic off, shirt sleeves rolled up, looking hot and irate, Sergeant Ramos stood scowling under the bright gleam of the cabin lights.

"*Boa tarde*, Sergeant," said Laird amiably. "Lost something?"

Ramos grunted, tossed aside a grubby canvas bag he'd been checking, and sat down on the bared wooden slats of the dead man's bunk.

"A police matter, Senhor Laird," he

said. "What do you want this time?"

"Call it a friendly visit," said Laird. He brought out his cigarettes, flipped one across to the man, took one for himself, and shared his lighter flame. "You said I could look through Soller's diving notes."

"Sim." Ramos gave a slight nod. He drew hard on his cigarette, then let the smoke out in a slow sigh. "I had forgotten. Yes, you can see them — if you can find them."

"I don't think I understand," said Laird carefully.

Ramos shrugged. "I can show you his bank book, his naval discharge papers, several indiscreet letters from women who should have known better, even his grocery bills. But there are no diving notes — none I can find, anyway."

"But that's not what you're looking for, is it?" asked Laird.

Slowly, Ramos shook his head.

"Then?" Laird waited.

"Suppose" — the man hesitated,

then seemed to make up his mind — "suppose this was your boat, Senhor Laird. Suppose you wished to hide — well, a number of articles, modest in size, certainly not large. What would you do?"

"First, I'd need to have an idea how important it was they weren't found," answered Laird. "What are we talking about, Sergeant?"

"*Por favor*, Senhor Laird, I am asking for help," said Ramos. He took another long draw from his cigarette, then mashed the rest of it to a pulp against one of the wooden slats beside him. "You are an expert on boats — "

"On insuring them, though some people have doubts about that," Laird corrected him. "Are you trying to tell me he was smuggling?"

Ramos shook his head. "Jorges Soller? He hadn't the brains. But if he had things to hide — "

"I can try," said Laird, cutting him short. "Where have you looked?"

"Everywhere." Ramos waved a hairy

hand in a weary gesture meant to encompass the entire boat. "Everywhere that seemed obvious. As for your diving notes, Senhor Laird, I have the feeling that someone else has already been searching through the *Juhno*. Perhaps that's why I can't find them."

"Sergeant, you don't make sense." Laird got to his feet, with the feeling of being lost in a maze. "But if he did have a built-in hideaway, the first rule is it should be simple — so simple that people ignore it."

He set to work, Ramos following him around like an overweight shadow, watching, saying nothing. For Laird, it was the reverse of the old game he'd seen played often enough at sea, when it was a matter of honour to try to outwit the Customs rummage squads when your ship arrived in port. Except then it had been mainly untaxed cigarettes or liquor, the occasional watch or camera, the basics for a run ashore.

The tiny forepeak was so grubby it had to be 'clean'. But he checked, then gradually worked aft from there. The cracked, faded panelling in the cabin sounded uniformly dull when tapped. In the wheelhouse, there was a small inspection panel under the wheel mounting. It slid open, and a half-emptied bottle of brandy toppled out.

That was all. Through the tiny engine room, squeezing beyond to the stern, going out on deck with the sudden memory of a bo'sun who had once made a hollow metal replica of a lifebuoy, Laird at last returned to the cabin.

"Sorry," he said flatly as Ramos slumped down on the bunk again.

"You tried," said the policeman. *"Obrigado."*

Then, suddenly, Laird realised he hadn't finished. He'd forgotten the very rule he'd given Ramos — look somewhere so simple you ignore it.

"Get up," he said sharply, staring at the bunk. It was a simple four-legged frame, screwed against the bulkhead. "Move — and find me a screwdriver."

For once, Ramos moved quickly. He was back in seconds with a long-handled screwdriver from the engine room tool kit. Laird took it and slid under the bunk, ignoring the scuttling cockroaches. Six large, apparently rusted screws held the bunk in place but they came out smoothly, their threads glinting with oil. They dragged the bunk out — and a neatly cut oblong hole was exposed in the bulkhead.

"Por favor . . . " Ramos almost pushed him aside, knelt down, and reached in. Face intent, he felt around, then one by one began bringing out an assortment of small packages, each wrapped in squares of old rags.

Five minutes later a magpie collection of articles lay unwrapped on the cabin table. Two sets of binoculars, a brass sextant, a hand compass, a couple of small chronometers, several transistor radios, a pocket calculator, an expensive-looking camera — Laird gave up, and faced Ramos.

"You expected this?" he asked.

Ramos nodded.

"What the hell's it all about?"

"Thefts from boats around the bay, thefts which have been going on for months," said Ramos. "They were never too big to cause real trouble, always at night, always when the crew were ashore or asleep." He shrugged, then held up a finger and thumb, well apart. "I have a file of complaints on my desk this thick. Jorges Soller was my main suspect — a scuba diver can work along a waterfront or swim out to a moorings. But I never had proof."

"And this lot?"

"The most recent." Ramos nodded at the collection on the table. "The camera was reported stolen from an American yacht — the sextant too. Luis Bandeira, a fishing skipper, lost two sets of binoculars last week. One of those radios looks the type stolen from the Dutchman who is bo'sun on the *Craig Michael*. It was taken from his cabin."

"I see." Laird rubbed a hand slowly

and appreciatively across his chin, the wild tendril of an idea he'd had earlier coming back into his mind but stronger this time, still too tangled and complex for him to understand fully. He looked at the items again. "Then, suddenly, Soller gets himself killed. Next thing, you say it looks as if someone searched his boat. Tell me a couple of things, Sergeant. When do you think that happened and what's the coincidence rate in this part of Portugal?"

"*Quero*, I — " Ramos stopped and chewed his thick lower lip defensively. "I need time to think. It looked like an accident." He gestured at the table. "And these — are any of them worth the life of a man?"

"That might depend on the way he got them, or what he saw in the process," said Laird. "Have you found his motorcycle yet?"

Ramos shook his head uncomfortably.

"Ask yourself why," suggested Laird. He walked over to the cabin door, then glanced back at Ramos, who was just standing where he'd left him, looking puzzled and unhappy. "You wanted time to think, Sergeant. I'd say you've a lot to think about."

He didn't go straight back to the Pousada Pico. Instead, he found another small bar in a side street further along, ordered a beer, then sat alone at a table sipping the drink, nursing the glass between his hands, and doing exactly what he'd suggested to Ramos.

Thinking. Going back over all the apparently disconnected bits and pieces that had happened to him in the less than two days since he'd arrived at Porto Esco. How much the *Craig Michael* mattered in it, if she did, he didn't know. The Clanmore office in London would be closed for the night and he decided to leave trying to contact Osgood Morris till the morning. Because whatever was wrong, it was wrong in Porto Esco.

Jorges Soller had agreed to do a survey dive for him and had died. But the dive wasn't likely to be the reason — he had to be right, Soller had to have stumbled across something in one of his thieving expeditions, maybe without even realising it. If his boat had been searched, if his diving notes had been taken, it had to be because his killer feared they might contain at least a hint.

A hint of what? Laird swore in a way that made the nearby barman blink.

He couldn't even be sure Soller had been murdered. The way that exhaust pipe had been split could have been accidental. Except — He saw the barman still watching him and grinned reassuringly.

Except somebody had tried to run him down with a truck. Somebody had followed when he'd gone with Kati Gunn to that hideaway cove, followed them carrying a gun and ready to use it.

Add Harry Novak's arrival on the scene and everything which that involved — this time he swore inwardly. Then he finished his beer, tossed some coins on the table, and went out into the gathering darkness.

He had one candidate, a choice compounded mainly of dislike, prejudice, and a hunch. Walking along, almost colliding with a strolling group of teenagers, he muttered an apology and hardly heard their sarcastic replies.

No, he had two candidates. They were José da Costa and his partner Bonner.

Whatever the hell was going on.

★ ★ ★

The restaurant in the Pousada Pico had a midweek attraction that night, one which had filled a few extra tables with nonresident customers. While a melancholy-faced guitarist rippled occasional chords from his instrument, a plump, full-busted female in the traditional black dress of her kind gave a recital of *fado* songs. *Fado* for sadness — her high, mournful voice dominated the softly lit room, drowned the clatter of cutlery, and was rewarded with a burst of applause each time she halted.

Andrew Laird went in to eat about eight o'clock, when the *fado* performance was in full flow. A waiter began to guide him across to a vacant table but he signalled the man to wait and stopped, staring, totally surprised at the occupants of another table near the door.

Harry Novak had shaved his scarred face and wore a clean shirt and tie. Opposite him, smiling quietly and listening to something he was saying, Mary Amos wore an off-the-shoulder print dress and had a small string of pearls round her plump throat. Her red hair had been brushed till it shone and she'd been using eye make-up.

"Good evening," said Laird with an effort.

"Good evening, Mr. Laird," she said, glancing up. "We were just talking about you — Captain Novak was telling me about when you used to sail together."

"That must have been interesting," said Laird sardonically. He glanced at the almost emptied bottle of wine on the table between them, then at Novak. "Enjoying yourself, Harry?"

Novak gave a feeble grin and emitted a mutter which was lost as the *fado* singer hit a new, penetrating note and held it. He tried again.

"I'm trying to square things — " he began.

"He is." Mary Amos's voice held a note of pleased satisfaction. "You can relax, Mr. Laird. Captain Novak has totally apologised for this afternoon. He explained he was — well, shall we say under considerable strain? Perhaps I took a little persuading, but in the end I accepted his apology — and dinner with him."

Laird swallowed hard. "How much persuading do you reckon your husband will need, Mrs. Amos?"

"John?" A slight frown showed for

162

a moment, then was gone. "Captain Novak intends to see him first thing in the morning." She smiled across the table. "Don't you, Captain?"

"First thing," echoed Novak dutifully. "Look, I lost the place out there. Amos needs me, I need him, so — "

"So you'd better go out there waving a white flag," said Laird. Deliberately, he prodded Novak in the stomach with a finger exactly where his punch had landed earlier and saw the man wince. "We wouldn't want any more misunderstandings, would we?"

"No." For a moment anger flared in Novak's eyes, then it subsided.

"However," said Mary Amos, as if she hadn't noticed anything, "I still think I'll stay ashore for a day or two, Mr. Laird — until the *Craig Michael* is refloated. After being stuck aboard ship for so long, I'm enjoying the change. And, of course, it makes John happier when so much will be going on out there."

"I'm sure you're right," said Laird.

"Enjoy your meal."

He nodded good-bye, saw the waiter still hovering, and let the man guide him over to a table halfway down the restaurant, where he was close enough to the *fado* singer to see that she needed some dental work and had nicotine staining on her fingers.

Ordering at random from the menu, Laird ate sparingly while the *fado* performance sobbed on. Now and again he took time for another, disbelieving glance over towards Novak and Mary Amos, who had a new bottle of wine on their table.

But whatever was going on, whatever kind of game either or both of them were playing, it was none of his business — he just hoped it would stay that way.

The *fado* singer, busy squeezing out a high note, gave him a surprising wink as he finally rose and left. At a guess, decided Laird, she was married to the guitar player and would have to cook supper for him when they got home.

That was life. He squeezed a way out through the tables, taking a route that avoided Novak and Mary Amos, went through the Pico's deserted lobby, and from there went up to his room.

He changed clothes quickly, from his white shirt and light-coloured suit to a dark sweater and slacks. Transferring money, a pocketknife, car keys, his cigarettes and lighter into the pockets of the slacks, he smiled as he caught his reflection in the mirror.

Laird left his room a moment later, closing the door quietly behind him, and went back down to the Pico's lobby. It was empty, and he crossed quickly to the exit. But as he went to step out into the night he collided with two figures intent on coming in.

"Hello there, Mr. Laird," said a cheerful, throaty voice. Andy Dawson's lined, elderly face was beaming, there was an early hint of liquor on his breath, and the *Craig Michael*'s engineer had Jody Cruft, the tanker's bo'sun, grinning at his side.

"Who let you two ashore?" said Laird good-naturedly. "I thought the Old Man would want you standing by to repel boarders."

"No way, Mr. Laird," said the Dutch bo'sun in his carefully accented English. "Captain Amos is sitting out there happy as can be wit' a bottle in one hand an' a shotgun in the other. He said go an' enjoy ourselves, that it might be the last time for a spell."

"Could be too," nodded Andy Dawson. "So Jody an' I thought that before we really got started we'd look in and see that Mrs. Amos was settled and happy."

"She is," said Laird, easing round slightly so that he blocked the doorway. "In fact, I saw her. She was going off to bed, having an early night. I wouldn't disturb her."

"She had one damn bad afternoon," said Jody Cruft solemnly. "An' she's a nice woman. If she's resting, that's fine."

"I'll tell her in the morning. She'll

166

appreciate it," Laird told them, relaxing again. "No more trouble with Novak or his people?"

"None." Andy Dawson shook his head. He gave a chuckle that sounded like rustling gravel. "Give me a chance and if there is a next time I'll play a steam hose on their backsides."

"An' it made a change," said Jody Cruft. "You know what people say about sailing in tankers, Mr. Laird — that it's as boring as being in jail wit' the added risk of drowning. It livened things up."

Laird nodded, a new thought in his mind. "By now, you two must know your way pretty well around Porto Esco, and most people in it. How about that character Bonner, from the shipbreaking yard? Any idea where he lives?"

"Da Costa's square-faced pal?" Dawson asked. "He has a cottage on the shore right on the south edge of town, towards Cabo Esco. He even has his own little private slipway there — you can't miss it."

"The other thing about being here all those months must be that you know everything that happens in that channel," said Laird. He paused deliberately. "Just normal fishing port traffic, I suppose. Or — well, ever see anything unusual going on?"

Dawson looked blank and shook his head. Then, suddenly, Jody Cruft gave the elderly engineer a good-natured cuff on the arm.

"You could always tell about that whale you imagined you saw a couple of months ago, an' how it scared the hell out of you," he suggested, grinning.

"Who imagined it?" protested Dawson indignantly. "It was so near I saw — "

"He saw the whites of its eyes," finished Cruft, and winked. "It was my birthday, Mr. Laird. So Andy an' I, we got beautifully drunk to celebrate. Then we get back out to the *Craig Michael*, late on, an' Andy insists he'll sleep on deck. Then next morning he insists he saw this whale, the biggest in the world, growling an' grunting an' looking straight at him as it went past."

"I saw it," said Dawson. "So maybe I was wrong about its size. But it was big all right — biggest I've ever seen."

"Like it could hardly get past us?" jeered Cruft. "Man, you were so stoned that night it was probably a sardine in disguise."

Dawson sniffed. "A whale's a whale. Nobody has to believe me." Then he frowned. "I thought we came ashore to do some drinking? If the captain's missus is okay, let's get to it."

They said good-bye and ambled back off into the night.

With an amused but thoughtful twinkle in his grey-green eyes, Laird watched them go. Then he started off across the courtyard to his car. But as he reached it the Pico's door opened and Kati Gunn came out.

"Andrew" — she hurried across to

join him — "good — I was looking for you."

"Suddenly, I'm in demand," said Laird, and looked her up and down approvingly. She wore a sleeveless white lace blouse over tailored blue slacks, the blouse fastened low by a heavy silver brooch. "Where have you been hiding?"

"Hiding is the word," Kati said wryly. "Every time I see Mama Isabel she wants to know what we did this afternoon." She paused and raised an eyebrow. "Think I should tell her?" Then she reached into the pocket of her slacks. "I've got a message for you, from Mrs. Amos — she made a trip to the powder room, saw me, and asked me to make sure you got it."

Laird took the little slip of folded paper from her. Opening it, he read the pencilled scribble by the soft glow of lights coming from the Pico.

"MR. L. THERE'S MORE THAN ONE WAY TO TEACH A MAN A LESSON. M.A."

170

He put the note in his pocket, then glanced at Kati.

"What's she up to in there?" he asked.

Kati shrugged. "I wouldn't have the nerve to ask."

"That makes two of us," he admitted. "Can you keep an eye on her?"

"She's old enough to be my mother," said Kati, startled.

"That's as good a reason as any," said Laird, grinning. "Will you?"

She sighed and nodded. "Do I get to ask what you'll be doing?"

Laird hesitated. He hoped he could trust her, he thought he could trust her, but an inner caution told him it was a bad moment to take chances.

"I've some driving to do," he lied. "I've a report and drawings that my London office needs in a hurry. If I get them to Faro airport, they'll be on the first plane out tomorrow."

He kissed her lightly on the lips, got into the Simca, and started the engine. She gave him a wave as he set the car

171

moving and was still there as he drove out of the courtyard.

Laird grimaced to himself. He wouldn't be going near Faro airport, but he had a few other places in mind.

5

THE night was dark and the shore road was quiet. But Andrew Laird still couldn't be sure he wasn't being watched and he drove the Simca north at first, as if heading for the Faro road, constantly checking his rearview mirror. Then, satisfied, he used a couple of side streets, returned to the shore road at a point well south of the Pousada Pico, and went in search of Charles Bonner's cottage.

He had reached the edge of Porto Esco and was beginning to have doubts about Andy Dawson's directions when the car head lamps showed an isolated house ahead. It was on the shore side of the road, set on a spit of land, and the thin finger of a small jetty showed as a black silhouette at the water's edge.

Laird drove past the cottage. About

a minute on, the road forked at a tiny roadside shrine. He took the right-hand fork, which was a narrow track, and stopped the Simca out of sight of the main road. Switching off lights and engine, he got out and walked back.

He paused at the shrine, a devout little structure defaced by a faded political poster, and let a car murmur past on the main road. Then, the only sound in the still, warm darkness the chirping of crickets, the scent of cactus challenging the sea tang of the bay, he headed for the cottage.

It had a large, overgrown patch of garden surrounded by a low boundary wall and though the cottage windows were in darkness a glow of light was visible from a big shed at the rear, close to the jetty. Keeping close to the wall, using it as cover, Laird worked his way along until he had a clear view of the jetty and the shed — then he stopped, crouching down, his lips shaping a silent whistle of interest.

The low, distinctive hull of the *Mama*

Isabel was lying beside the jetty and Charles Bonner had just emerged from the shed, carrying a crate which clinked as he marched along with it. He reached the jetty, loaded the crate aboard the launch, and started back again. Another figure emerged from the shed at the same time — da Costa, carrying a similar, clinking crate, which he also put aboard the launch.

Each man made another couple of similar trips. Then Bonner, coming out with yet another crate, stumbled as he reached the jetty. He dropped the crate, Laird heard glass break, Bonner swearing softly, and da Costa chuckling as he came to help.

The crate was loaded aboard like the rest. The two men went back together, made one more trip carrying a bigger, differently shaped container between them, then Bonner went back to the shed alone.

The light went out, the door creaked shut, and Bonner returned to the launch, stooping to untie a mooring line before he stepped aboard. The engine fired, settled immediately to a low purr, and the *Mama Isabel* eased away, a shadow in the night which vanished as she headed out across the bay in the direction of the twinkling lights that marked the channel to the Companhia Tecnico yard.

Laird rose from hiding, vaulted the low wall, and crossed through the tangle of long grass towards the shed. A dull white pool of liquid marked the spot where Bonner had stumbled and several fragments of broken glass bottle lay in the middle of the liquid. Puzzled, Laird stooped beside the stain, tested it with his fingers, then raised a finger to his lips.

It was milk, plain, ordinary milk.

Bewildered now, he went on to the shed. The door was locked but a small window at the side had the kind of catch which only needed a moment's work with a penknife blade. Laird swung it open, climbed through into the pitch black darkness, and used the flame of his cigarette lighter to locate the light switch.

Two bare electric bulbs came to life when he flicked the switch. They shone down on Bonner's big cream Range-Rover, which occupied about a third of the interior. Laird ignored it, his eyes on a motorcycle which lay propped against the wall near the door. One glance told him it wasn't Jorges Soller's missing machine. This one was smaller, an Italian lightweight with heavy duty motorcross-style tyres for cross-country work — and Soller's machine had also had that skeleton sidecar. But he examined it closely. The frame and wheels were thick with a yellow grit like the surface of the dirt road which led to the beach where he and Kati had been spied on.

Mouth tightening, Laird began checking around the rest of the shed. It had the usual workbench space, cupboards holding an assortment of tools and tins, everything to be expected in a combined boathouse and garage.

But he found a small, almost empty bottle of gun oil on the workbench, beside some used cleaning rags. A cleared space near the door showed where the crates now on the *Mama Isabel* had been stacked, and a crumpled, torn scrap of paper lying at the corner of the door caught his eyes.

Picking it up, smoothing it out, he frowned over a column of figures which were apparently part of an adding machine's print roll. Then, shrugging, he stuffed the scrap of paper in his pocket and continued his search.

The Range-Rover yielded nothing, the rest of the shed was equally innocent, and he gave up. Switching out the lights, he left the window way he had entered, used his penknife blade to ease the catch shut again, and returned to the car.

Then, sitting behind the wheel, he lit a cigarette and sat for a moment, thinking. The wild idea which had been in his mind since that afternoon had become a positive hunch, though still without a basic peg to hang it on. It was one he had to follow through and the only place he could do that was at the Companhia Tecnico yard.

Taking another draw on the cigarette, he flicked the rest of it out of the driver's window. Starting the car, he reversed back to the little roadside shrine, swung out onto the main road, and set off round the bay.

* * *

Twenty minutes later, standing just inside the shelter of a patch of scrub pine, Andrew Laird looked across at the closed main gate of the Companhia Tecnico yard. A jumble of black outlined against the night, the yard looked deserted — but when he strained his ears against the soft murmur of the wind he could hear the low, steady beat of an engine, coming from somewhere on the other side of the high perimeter fence. A moment earlier, he had seen the brief glow of a match as a guard standing in the shadow of a small hut inside the gate had lit a cigarette.

Something was certainly going on inside the shipbreaking yard, something the rest of Porto Esco wasn't meant to know about.

Laird looked at the perimeter fence again, thoughtfully. The yellow Simca was concealed back down the road, drawn in behind another patch of scrub, and he had Captain Amos's rusted Smith and Wesson .38 in his waistband, though what would happen if he had to pull the trigger was anybody's guess.

The fence was high and topped with barbed wire. Though the night was dark, anyone trying the climb would be conspicuous if by chance there was another guard on patrol — and there was always the possibility of being hooked on the barbs.

A small, unseen animal rustled away through the underbrush behind him and Laird grinned, feeling that for the moment they shared something in common. Animals seldom climbed fences — they had sense enough to look for a way under them.

He eased a little way along from the gate, then quit the shelter of the pines. His dark clothing blending into the night, he reached the edge of the fence, got down on his hands and knees, and began working along it. About a dozen fence posts on he found what he wanted — a narrow gap between the bottom edge of the fencing wire and a slight dip in the ground, a gap almost hidden by grass and weeds. It was a tight squeeze but he wriggled through, paused, then crawled quickly to the shelter of a pile of rusted steel plating.

Laird got to his feet, took his bearings from the black outlines of the yard cranes, then froze back into the shadows, left arm up to hide the white of his face, as a figure came strolling out of the night, patrolling along the inside edge of the fence.

The man passed by, humming softly, confident, near enough for Laird to see the unlit flash lamp he was carrying in one hand.

Laird let one full minute pass once he was out of sight, then set off. Skirting more dumps of metal and the vague outlines of equipment, he reached the long, low shape of the office block. A chink of light showed behind one curtained window, but the engine noise had become louder and was his main interest.

A silent-moving shadow, he passed by the main slipway, then the quayside where the yard's old tug boat lay creaking gently at her mooring ropes. The sound had become the air-gulping purr of a diesel engine, somewhere not far ahead, out of sight, but where the lapping water of the bay glinted at the start of an inlet he hadn't noticed before. The rest of his view was blocked by a long, brick-built shed — and between him and the shed was another wire fence, as high as the first

182

one and this time bedded firmly into concrete.

But it had a gate big enough to let a truck pass through, and the gate was ajar. Carefully, Laird scanned the night, then, every sense alert, suddenly dry-lipped and tempted to turn back, he slipped through.

He paused inside the gate. Nothing happened. Moistening his lips, his grip tightening on Amos's revolver, he went on and rounded the edge of the shed.

Then he stopped short, staring at the scene in front of him, at the same time hardly able to believe his eyes, yet so many things making sense.

He was on the edge of another small quay. Beyond it, the inlet from the bay glinted deep and wide — around the low, black hull of a submarine, the engine throb coming from its diesels, dimmed lights moving around the base of its squat, sail-shaped conning tower and da Costa's *Mama Isabel* lying beside it like a toy while tiny figures moved between launch and submarine.

There was something strange about the submarine's outline which took him a moment longer to realise.

It lay awkwardly, listing to one side, the bow low in the water, part of a long gash visible along its hull. Laird swallowed hard. He'd found old Andy Dawson's 'whale', he'd found the reason why Jorges Soller had been killed, why the *Craig Michael* had to be wrenched out of the Cabo Esco channel. The crates of milk and the other boxes he'd seen loaded on the *Mama Isabel* made sense now too, fresh and probably badly needed provisions for the submarine's crew.

He didn't really hear anything behind him, he was only suddenly conscious of not being alone. Then, before he could turn, something hard and heavy smashed down on his head and the world became a roaring red vortex for a brief instant of pain before he blacked out.

★ ★ ★

When he came round, all Laird could be sure of at first was that a light seemed to be shining straight down into his eyes, that his head ached, and that he could hear voices. Then, gradually, his blurred senses began to function again.

He was lying on his back, on a concrete floor, and the light came from a neon tube on the roof overhead. Moving his head slightly, he stifled a moan at the fresh stab of pain that caused — and the voices stopped. A moment later, a foot kicked him hard in the side.

"*Sim*, he's with us," rasped a voice.

Laird moved again, discovering in the process that his hands were tied in front of him, lashed tightly at the wrists. He looked up as a grinning, pock-marked face peered down at him. It was Miguel, the young, paunchy thug who had tried to make trouble with him that first night at the Pico's bar.

"Pick him up," said da Costa's voice.

"Lend a hand, Pedro."

The scrawny, unshaven fisherman who had been Miguel's companion moved in. The two men unceremoniously heaved Laird upright and dumped him into a sitting position on a crate. Still dazed, Laird saw he was inside the brick-built shed. A large number of crates and boxes were stacked carefully along one wall and a small group of men stood round him.

"Senhor Laird, you're a damned, interfering fool," said José da Costa in a soft, yet grim voice. Da Costa, his handsome, tanned face strangely pallid under the neon light, swung round to the men beside him. "*Não-sei* . . . if we could be sure there was no one else — "

"There won't be." Charles Bonner took a step forward, his expression stony. Then, suddenly, he hit Laird back-handed across the mouth and glared at him for a moment. "Miguel saw no one else, we've got his car — and you heard that oaf Novak call

186

him a troublemaking loner."

"So we gamble on it?" Da Costa looked unhappy.

There was a third man with them, a stranger who stood a few paces back. He was about Laird's age, he was dressed in a white roll-neck sweater, dark blue slacks and rope-soled canvas shoes, and he watched tight-lipped, saying nothing. Clean-shaven, with short, fair hair, there were tired lines on his face — and as his eyes met Laird's something close to sympathy showed for an instant. Then, very deliberately, he turned away.

"What's your problem, da Costa?" Laird heard his own voice come like a croak but somehow forced a grin. "Suppose I say I've got Sergeant Ramos and a squad of *policia* outside the main gate? Will that make you happy?"

"Ramos?" Da Costa glanced at Bonner. "No, we know where he is — "

"And what he's doing." Bonner completed it for him and gave a coarse laugh. "Same night every week, right, José?"

Da Costa scowled but nodded with relief.

"Thank God for middle-aged Romeos." Bonner grinned this time, but with little humour. "No, I reckon you're our only problem, Laird. I don't know what brought you here, but you've seen too much."

"That's my hard luck." Laird had the salt taste of blood in his mouth but his mind was still clearing. Clearing enough to let him realise that the way he had played things there was no chance of outside help. He nodded past Bonner and da Costa, towards the stranger. "Do I get introduced to your sea-going friend?"

"He prefers to stay out of this," said da Costa.

"I don't blame him," said Laird wearily. "He's commanding the original ship in a bottle — and I can think of happier places than a leaking submarine, particularly one that has to stay submerged most of the time. Any harm in my asking how it got dented?"

"Trying to get out of the channel on the night of the storm," said Bonner. "You're right, of course. The captain can't get out of the bay until your damned *Craig Michael* is moved, and his hull damage makes that urgent."

"Embarrassing too," suggested Laird. "But you've been taking care of things. What's it all about?"

Bonner and da Costa exchanged a glance which was hard to interpret. He heard the two fishermen behind him stir uneasily. Then, without answering, Bonner signalled to da Costa. Leaving Laird with his guards, they crossed the concrete floor to where the fair-haired submarine commander was waiting and began a low-voiced conversation.

Laird's head still throbbed. Moving his wrists, he managed to get a glance at his watch and sighed. It was close on midnight, which meant a couple of hours had passed since he had left the Pousada Pico. How long he'd been unconscious he couldn't be certain, but it must have been around half an hour.

The cord tying his wrists was painfully tight. He tried to ease it and was rewarded with an immediate cuff across the head from the paunchy Miguel.

Shrugging, Laird contented himself with another glance around the shed. It had no windows and a steel door, but the stacked boxes and crates interested him most. Bare of identification except for stencilled code markings, none were large and all looked capable of being manhandled. Their shapes . . . he sucked a sudden breath of understanding, then Bonner and da Costa were coming back, the fair-haired submarine commander staying where he was with his lips pursed tightly and the same odd expression of sympathy on his face.

"Pedro." Bonner pushed the unshaven little fisherman forward. "You've still got his car keys?"

The man nodded.

"Put the rest of his stuff back in his pockets. Miguel will take the old revolver he was carrying."

Pedro produced Laird's cigarettes and lighter and obeyed.

"The money too," said Bonner. He waited till that had also been returned, then eyed Laird dispassionately. "When you left Porto Esco you said you were driving to Faro. Well, it's a difficult road by night — I'm afraid you didn't make it."

Da Costa frowned a protest. "I still say I could take him out tomorrow night, on the run — "

"And first he disappears, then we risk him being washed up somewhere?" Bonner shook his head. "We'll keep it simple."

"Was that how it was with Jorges Soller?" asked Laird, the last remnant of hope he'd retained fading. Only Kati could have told them he was going to Faro, and what that implied was just one more body-blow towards despair. "I suppose you arranged his little accident too?"

Bonner's eyes narrowed, then he nodded.

"Why?" asked Laird.

"Because he came here thieving," said Bonner. "He used his scuba gear to swim round past the fence, broke into the office, and stole a few things. He was spotted as he left — that was the night before you arrived in Porto Esco." He paused and shrugged. "We didn't know how much he'd seen, but we figured that if he was curious he'd be back the next night. So, as you say, we arranged his little accident. Afterwards we found his motorcycle just about the same place you left your car tonight."

"Then you raided his boat to get his diving notes," said Laird.

"*Sim*, the notes and anything else that might point our way," said da Costa. "It happens there was nothing we would have worried about — but we never take risks."

"Angola taught us that," said Bonner harshly. He switched his glance to the two fishermen. "His car, the Faro road, and I want it to look like an accident. You know what to do?"

"*Sim*, Senhor Bonner," said Miguel. "There is a good spot three, maybe four kilometres out of Porto Esco. But — ah — *por favor*, how do we get back?"

"On your own flat feet. Just head home and stay there," said Bonner. He glanced at Laird again, shrugged, and turned away.

The two fishermen heaved Laird upright and shoved him towards the door. Da Costa went with them, opened it, and Laird saw the Simca outside. A man carrying a rifle was standing nearby and another couple of shadowy figures waited further back.

"*Adeus*, Senhor Laird," said da Costa. His white teeth flashed in the night. "You know, you and Kati were quite fascinating on that beach together. But maybe I should just have put a

193

bullet in you then."

Turning, Laird tried to take a swing at him with his bound hands. But da Costa side-stepped, still grinning, and Miguel slammed Laird hard against the car. Then he was bundled into the rear seat and Miguel climbed in beside him, jamming Amos's rusty Smith and Wesson .38 in his ribs, while Pedro got in behind the wheel.

Da Costa stood back, nodded, and Pedro started the car. They moved slowly, without lights, until they reached the gate in the outer perimeter fence. The man waiting there swung it open, then closed it again immediately after the car had gone through.

Whistling tunelessly through his teeth, Pedro changed gear, swung the wheel, and switched on the lights as they bounced onto the empty road.

"Relax, senhor," he said over his shoulder. "Miguel will tell you I am a good driver."

The two men laughed as the car began travelling.

For the first couple of kilometres the road stayed empty apart from a truck which lumbered past, heading in towards Porto Esco. Pedro kept up his tuneless whistling and drove unhurriedly while Miguel sat silent and Laird stayed equally quiet, doing his best to project a picture of total resignation.

But he was thinking hard. He knew the answer now to what it was all about. Gun-running — the crates and boxes back in that shed were identical to the types he'd seen in legitimate small arms and ammunition shipments, except for their lack of markings. Gun-running, but with major overtones.

He glanced at the man beside him and immediately felt the gun against his side increase its pressure. His lips tightened. Somehow, there had to be a chance left — and when it came up, he'd have to take it, fast and hard. What he'd fallen into was no ordinary smuggling operation and Bonner and da Costa were very obviously only the local connection. But they were ruthless, and so were the men who worked for them.

The narrow road began to climb and wind in the head lamps' glare, the earlier trees thinning and giving way to barren slopes. A wooden guardrail appeared on one side, the road partly hacked out of a shoulder of living rock.

Suddenly, he heard Pedro grunt and saw him nod towards the rearview mirror. Another car was coming up behind them, travelling fast, its lights drawing nearer as it closed the gap.

"Policia?" asked Miguel anxiously, glancing round.

Pedro shrugged. He had stopped whistling and was giving the rearview mirror as much attention as he could. In a few seconds the car was close behind them and its head lamps flashed impatiently.

"A woman," said Pedro with

undisguised relief, looking again in his mirror. "*Sim* . . . and on her own. I'll let her pass."

He slowed a little and drew the Simca tighter in towards the side of the road. With another flash of head lamps the car, a small black Volkswagen, swept past, the woman aboard a mere hunched shape behind the wheel. In another moment it had vanished round the next bend ahead.

Grinning, Pedro winked in the rearview mirror at his companion and relaxed. But seconds later, as they rounded still another bend, he swore hard and jammed on the brakes.

The black Volkswagen had stopped broadside across the road just ahead, lights still blazing, door lying open and a limp figure in a headscarf and gaberdine coat slumped against it, halfway out of the car.

Tyres squealing, the Simca skidded to a halt with only a couple of car lengths to spare. Still cursing, Pedro threw open his door and got out — while Laird stifled a gasp. The woman's face was hidden, but the Simca's lights caught a glint of tawny hair escaping from the head scarf.

Pedro was halfway across, obscuring Laird's view, when something seemed to click in Miguel's mind. Grabbing for his door, he threw it open and gave a warning bellow. For an instant, the revolver swung away from Laird's side and that was enough. Slamming sideways across the seat, Laird hurled against the man with a pile-driving force which knocked him out of the car and sprawling on the roadway.

The gun in Miguel's hand blasted harmlessly, skyward, then Laird had jumped after him, knees smashing into the man's chest. A scream and another shot came from the direction of the VW, but Miguel, retching with pain, was still bringing the revolver up again.

Bound hands clenched together, Laird took a full-arm swing which had every ounce of his weight behind it. The hammer-like blow took Miguel just below the ear with a crunch of shattering bone. The man gave one convulsive jerk and a strange, gobbling sigh, then collapsed, the .38 falling from his grasp.

Diving sideways, Laird grabbed the weapon and pivoted round in a desperate half-roll, thinking of Pedro and Kati, ready to fire.

But there was no need. Kati was leaning against the Volkswagen's side, her face white in the Simca's head lamps, a small automatic still tightly clenched in her right hand while she stared down at the shape lying huddled at her feet. Getting up, Laird saw for himself. They didn't have to worry about Pedro. Nobody did. The neat, round bullet hole just below one eye and the broad exit wound at the back of his skull had made certain of that for all time.

"He had a knife," said Kati, her voice dull and toneless. "He — "

"He would have killed you," said Laird firmly. "You stopped him. Keep it at that." He showed her the way his wrists were still bound. "We could use his knife."

She nodded, but didn't move. Tossing Amos's old .38 into the Volkswagen, Laird bent over Pedro again and took the razor-edged fish-gutting knife still clasped in the man's right fist. Then he went back to Kati.

"Cut me loose," he said quietly.

She laid the little automatic beside the other gun, took the knife, and the keen, curved blade sliced through the cords. As they fell away, Laird closed his eyes for a moment while his circulation made an agonising recovery. Then, rubbing the deep weals on his wrists, he went back to where Miguel lay.

The paunchy fisherman's eyes were staring unblinkingly at the night, his head twisted at a grotesque, unnatural angle. Laird winced, remembering the terrible, desperate hammer blow he'd used, feeling again the crunch of bone, realising he'd broken the man's neck.

He looked back at Kati, who had turned away and was leaning her head on her arms against the Volkswagen, as if trying to shut out the reality of what was around her.

Sighing, Laird took stock while a light breeze sprang up and rustled the long grass which clung between the rocks at one side of the road. On the other — he went over to the wooden guardrail, looked down into a black emptiness, then picked up a pebble and tossed it over. He heard it bounce and rattle down for what seemed a long time. Then, his mind made up, he went back to Kati.

"They're both dead," he said quietly. "Kati, I've got to win myself some time. That means tidying things here, fast — before anyone else comes along." Gently, he put his hands on her shoulders and brought her round to face him. "Tell me one thing first. How much do you know?"

She shook her head dumbly.

"Then how — ?" He left it unfinished.

"José phoned me from the yard, wanting to know where you were," she said. "When I said Faro airport, he — well, there was just something about the way he spoke. I knew something was terribly wrong."

"So you drove out to the yard?"

She nodded. "I took Mama Isabel's car. The gun is one she keeps in the office." Stopping, she bit her lip. "Then I waited near the yard gate and saw these two leaving with you. I — well, I just followed, I just knew I had to do something."

"You did." Laird touched her lips with a forefinger. "Now it's my turn. Get your car in off the road, beside the rocks. Like I said, I've got to tidy things."

Her eyes widened in horror. "But — "

"It makes no difference to them," said Laird.

She nodded, got into the Volkswagen and started it. Turning away, Laird dragged each of the two dead men in turn to the Simca, dumped Pedro in the front passenger seat, and deposited his companion in the rear. By the time he'd finished, Kati had moved the Volkswagen clear but stayed in it, just watching.

Reaching into the Simca, he started the engine, left it idling in neutral, and turned the steering wheel until the front wheels were angled towards the fence. Then he released the hand brake, closed the driver's door, went round to the back of the little car, and began pushing.

Head lamps lighting the way, it rolled forward gathering speed and hit the wooden fence rail with a snapping crunch. Both front wheels went over the edge, the rest of the car seemed to balance like a seesaw, then it slowly toppled and slid over.

Standing at the edge, Laird watched as the car crashed and bounced down into the depths of the rocky gorge. When it hit the bottom, one taillight was still glowing.

Then it went out — and a second

later a blast of flame erupted as the fuel tank exploded.

He stayed there a few seconds longer, watching the car burning like a torch far below. Then he went back to the Volkswagen, eased Kati over into the passenger seat, got behind the wheel himself, and lit a cigarette for each of them. His hands were trembling.

"We're going back into Porto Esco," he told her, starting the engine. "There's one man there who can help me — whether he likes it or not."

★ ★ ★

A drunk on a donkey cart was the sum total of traffic they passed on the way back to the bay. Her face a faint silhouette in the soft glow from the instrument panel, Kati listened quietly while Laird talked. He told her exactly what had happened from the time he'd left the Pico that night and when he finished she stayed silent for a moment, hands clasped in her lap, her eyes on the road ahead.

"Mama Isabel has been good to me," she said slowly. "If she was involved — "

"It doesn't look that way," Laird assured her. "All right, José is her son. So it's going to be rough for her." He shrugged. "Right now, that's almost incidental. But you've got her car and her gun. What happens if she or José find that out?"

"They won't," she said confidently. "José said he was staying with Bonner tonight — he won't be back." She paused and gave a slight smile. "As for Mama Isabel, this is the one night of the week when I can guarantee she's otherwise engaged."

"Sergeant Ramos?" asked Laird, and grinned when she nodded. "How long does he stay?"

"Till about 2 A.M., then he uses a back way out of the courtyard. He lives at the *policia* station."

The lights of Porto Esco were starting

to show ahead. Laird hummed under his breath, the rest of his idea firming.

"Anyone else likely to be at the police station at this hour?"

"No. It's only manned till midnight. His two constables live out."

"Good," said Laird.

Though, with what he had in mind, he felt almost sorry for the wooden-faced policeman.

* * *

Manuel Ramos was certainly a creature of habit. It was seconds after 2 A.M. when the Pousada Pico's courtyard door was quietly opened.

Standing well back in the dark shadow of the narrow little alleyway which ran from the rear of the courtyard, the night now chill enough for his feet to feel cold, Andrew Laird gave a grunt of relief as he watched the figures of Ramos and Mama Isabel exchange a fond farewell in the unlit doorway.

Then Mama Isabel, a small, slim figure in a long white dressing gown, went back inside and the door closed. Lighting one of his thin cigars, Sergeant Ramos stayed in the doorway a moment longer, then ambled towards the alleyway. He was out of uniform, wearing a close-fitting sweater and slacks.

"*Boa noite*, Sergeant," said Laird dryly, stepping out of the shadows at the last moment. "Been enjoying yourself?"

Sergeant Ramos swallowed hard, taken aback, and nodded.

"Good," said Laird, coming closer. Then he frowned. "Sergeant, you forgot to fasten your fly."

"*Obrigado,*" said Ramos in a confused mutter, glancing down. "I — "

He stopped there, eyes goggling, as Laird jammed the rusty .38 into his side.

"It's a big gun, Sergeant," murmured Laird. "I'd hate to use it. So just shut up and move."

He propelled the policeman along the alleyway to where it emerged in the dim lamplight of a back street. The Volkswagen was parked there, with Kati behind the wheel, and she leaned across and opened the passenger door.

"*Por favor*, into the back seat, Sergeant," said Laird. "We're giving you a lift home."

Gulping, Ramos obeyed. Laird climbed in beside him, closing the door, and Kati set the little car moving. Then, and only then, Ramos released a splutter of angry indignation.

"Senhor Laird, what you are doing is — is — "

"A serious offence," agreed Laird helpfully.

Licking his lips, Ramos tried again. "This is banditry." He leaned forward. "Senhorita Kati, if your aunt knew about this — "

"She wouldn't approve," finished Kati. Then her eyes met the policeman's in the rearview mirror and for a moment her manner changed. "Manuel, it may not look like it but we need your help. Maybe my aunt will need it too — and soon. So do what you're told, please."

Still spluttering, but even more bewildered, Sergeant Ramos sat on the edge of the seat and scowled until they reached the police station. It was in darkness and Kati stopped the Volkswagen round at the rear, in the shadow of the mortuary block. They got out and, prodded on by the .38 in Laird's hand, Sergeant Ramos unlocked a side door.

"Your office," ordered Laird, then stopped the man as he fumbled for a light switch. "No, not till the shades are closed."

They waited while Kati shut the blinds, then, the lights on, Ramos glared at them as they stood in the middle of his tiny office.

"Tell me this man is mad," he pleaded to Kati. "Because, if he is not — "

"Sit down, Sergeant," said Laird, cutting him short. Then, as Ramos subsided angrily in a chair, he went over to the telephone on the man's desk. "Sergeant, I've still got this gun and you're a big target. But listen to me. I'm going to make a phone call. It concerns some people who almost certainly think I'm dead by now — and if they find out differently they're not going to be happy about it. But once I've made that phone call I've got the insurance I need — and when it comes to insurance, I'm a believer."

Ramos moistened his lips again and scowled.

"*Sim*, you have to be mad," he said. "Kati — "

His voice faltered and died. Kati had taken the chair opposite him and had produced Mama Isabel's little revolver from her coat pocket. It was trained firmly on Ramos's ample middle.

"Manuel, let me tell you just how real all this is," she said quietly. "There are two dead men in a burned-out car off the Faro road. They helped kill Jorges Soller. Now shut up."

★ ★ ★

The international telephone trunk line network is usually stress-free around 2 A.M. and Laird's call to Osgood Morris's home in London connected in a matter of seconds. But then the number rang for over a minute before the sleepy voice of the Clanmore Alliance marine claims manager finally answered.

"Good God, do you know what time it is?" he protested when he heard Laird's greeting. "Look, you've even wakened my wife — "

"Send her back to her basket, Osgood," said Laird dryly. "Sorry, but this is urgent."

"Urgent?" Morris needed a moment for that to sink in. "If it's the *Craig Michael* — "

"Yes and no," said Laird. He grimaced at Kati and saw Sergeant Ramos was listening hard, trying to follow. "I need help, Osgood. You may have to get the chairman to shove

211

his weight behind this. To start with, several people think I'm dead — "

"You're dead drunk," snarled Morris. "I'll ignore that insult to my wife, but I'm going to hang up."

"I'm stone cold sober but I'm sitting holding a gun on the local sergeant of *policia*," said Laird wearily. "I don't like it, he doesn't like it. So phone some of your prize contacts at the Ministry of Defence — and the chairman knows a few admirals. Tell them the reason there's a rush to get the *Craig Michael* heaved out of the Cabo Esco channel is there's a submarine trapped in the bay. I saw her, she's damaged, and there's what looks like a miniature arsenal of weapons hidden in a warehouse ashore."

There was a long pause on the line.

"You're serious?" asked Morris.

"I'm serious," said Laird.

"Then be careful," said Morris. "We found out more about the *Craig Michael* charter. We're positive now that it is being done through the

Russian trade legation in London. So — "

"So you'd better take a note of this number." Laird gave him the police station number. "Tell your friends I need someone high-powered and Portuguese to call me back, and quickly — someone my friend the sergeant won't argue with."

He hung up, sighed, and found Ramos was staring at him.

"Senhor Laird, my English is not too good," said Ramos carefully. "But, *por favor* — what you said just now was true?"

Laird nodded.

"Obrigado," said the stolid-faced policeman sadly. Then he heaved himself to his feet, ignored Laird's faint warning gesture with the .38, and opened a cupboard. Taking out a bottle of brandy, he shrugged. "If we have to wait, it can be in comfort."

Exactly twenty minutes passed before the telephone rang. Sergeant Ramos answered it, then nodded to Laird and handed him the receiver.

"I'll keep it short, Mr. Laird," said the crisp, calm, and friendly voice at the other end of the line. "I'm calling from Lisbon. We have mutual friends in London who tell me you've got problems. Uh — things haven't got any worse?"

"Not yet," said Laird.

The voice chuckled. "We're very interested. Do you mind staying dead for a spell?"

"If that's what you want," agreed Laird.

"Yes." For a moment, the other man held a quick, low-voice conversation with someone else at his end, then he came back. "We want you to stay put, lie low, and do absolutely nothing for the next few hours. A couple of our people will arrive around noon — we've a few things to sort out between times. You understand?"

"Totally."

"Then put Sergeant Ramos on. Someone wants to talk to him."

Wordlessly, Laird passed the receiver to Ramos. As the policeman listened he suddenly stiffened, then, eyes widening, shoulders going back, he stood like a soldier on parade. Then, with a muted murmur, he finally replaced the receiver and took a quick swallow from his brandy glass.

"Well?" asked Kati impatiently.

"I have orders to — to totally assist Senhor Laird." Ramos drew a deep breath. "They come direct from the office of the President. He — they even knew about my army service, down to the name of my platoon commander." He turned to Laird. "I apologize, Senhor Laird. I said you were mad — maybe it is the whole world that has gone that way."

"Join the club," said Laird. "Now I'm going to tell you what we know, Sergeant — before you give me a bed in your best cell for the night and you make sure Kati gets back to the Pico without problems." He paused and twisted a grin. "Incidentally, I hope

215

you're a good liar. I want that burned-out car found before dawn — and I want everyone to hear there were three bodies in it, not two."

Ramos nodded solemnly, reached for the brandy bottle, topped up his glass, and emptied it at a swallow.

"You know something, Senhor Laird?" he asked sadly. "I was never much good at arithmetic."

6

THE police cell block at Porto Esco ran little risk of top rating in any tourist guide. But Andrew Laird was tired enough to have slept on a plank and he didn't even bother to read the graffiti on the walls before he slumped down on his bunk's straw mattress and pulled the blankets over him.

When he wakened, Sergeant Ramos was standing over him, shaking his shoulder, and the sun was pouring in through the small iron-barred window set high above them.

"Bom dia," said Ramos with a dry, lopsided grin. "Would you like to rise from the dead, Senhor Laird?" He nodded towards a laden tray lying on the cell table. "I brought you some breakfast."

"Thanks." Yawning, Laird swung his

legs out from under the blankets, sat on the edge of the bunk, and discovered in the process that his head still protested at sudden movement. It was 9 A.M. by his watch and a low murmur of traffic outside showed that the rest of Porto Esco was already well into the new day. Then the significance of Ramos's words sank in. "Where am I supposed to be right now?"

"In the mortuary at Tavira, the first decent-sized town between here and Faro airport," said Ramos while Laird pulled on his shirt and slacks. He shrugged. "*Sim*, it seems that a few people received surprise telephone calls from Lisbon during the night. It was all arranged. My report book shows that a burned-out car was discovered by a passing motorist on the road to Faro soon after dawn. He told the police when he got to Taviro, they advised me they would handle it, and three bodies were found in the car."

"Good." Laird went over to the tray. It held coffee, bacon and eggs, and thickly buttered chunks of bread. Feeling surprisingly hungry, he began eating. "Did you go out?"

Ramos nodded soberly. "When they moved the bodies. It was — well, not pleasant. A burning car makes a good incinerator." He helped himself to a chunk of bread and chewed it pensively. "Still, no one is likely to question what happened apart from our local *médico* — he will be annoyed at losing his autopsy fees."

"As long as I'm decently dead." Laird tasted the coffee, winced, and decided the Porto Esco police would never make a fortune out of room service. How about your two constables?"

"Both out on patrol in the town, and they know nothing. Then, of course, I also went *imediatamente* to the Pousada Pico and broke the sad news of your death. Everyone was most upset — "

"That's nice to know," murmured Laird.

"I asked them to pack your bag," said

Ramos doggedly. "Then I suggested that Kati bring it here, so that we could hold your belongings until we heard from your next of kin — who would pay the bill you left behind."

"You look after everyone's interests," said Laird.

"I try. Senhor, when you finish eating you'll find my quarters down the corridor, on the left. I have a spare razor you can use, then I would like you to stay there, out of sight. There's a chance I may have visitors."

Laird nodded, then considered the bulky man sympathetically.

"Awkward for you, isn't it, Sergeant?" he said quietly.

Ramos sucked his lips and gave an embarrassed nod.

"Mama Isabel." Laird sighed. "I told you last night I didn't think she was involved."

"So I just lie to her," said Ramos. "And the lies are just a start — José is her son."

"But there's no other way," said
Laird.

Ramos nodded gloomily and went
out.

★ ★ ★

Twenty minutes later, washed and
shaved, Andrew Laird peered out
through the slatted blind which covered
the window in Sergeant Ramos's room
and knew the first, early symptoms of
impatience.

The view was across the sunlit roofs
of Porto Esco towards the tantalising
sparkle of the water in the bay. But
whatever else was happening, all he
could see was a solitary fishing boat.

Turning away, he knew that for
the moment he was trapped just as
surely as if he'd been locked up in
one of those cells along the corridor
— and glancing round Ramos's room
the difference in comfort was only a
degree more than minimal. It could
have been lifted straight out of an

infantry barracks in its bare simplicity. The policeman had a bed and an armchair, a wardrobe and a wash-basin. His best uniform was hanging on a peg behind the door and the most personal item in the room was a small unsigned photograph of Isabel da Costa, which sat on top of the locker.

Shrugging, he lit one of his few remaining cigarettes, sank down in the chair, and frowned at the ceiling. Being officially dead had its disadvantages, but at least it did give him time to think, to get a cool, clear grip on the reality of what was happening.

Somewhere out there, under the blue water of the bay, one damaged submarine lay trapped. Her crew were prisoners too, with no escape for their craft until the Cabo Esco channel was cleared.

And it had been that way with them for over a week. He grimaced, remembering the tired face of the fair-haired submarine commander and guessing at the stresses and tensions which must be building up with each passing day.

But the submarine was still, in basic terms, only an apparent delivery truck. Ignoring the gaps, Laird tried to piece the rest of it together in his mind while a tiny fly buzzed around the cool shade of the room.

The apparently peaceful little town outside the window was the base for a gun-running operation, to customers unknown. A fast launch like the *Mama Isabel* was an ideal craft when it came to distribution, and the Companhia Tecnico yard was an equally ideal base — with its daytime work force probably totally unaware of what was going on.

But Jorges Soller had been a risk to that situation, and had died. Laird knew he'd come within a hairsbreadth of ending up the same way — and a lot now depended on how Bonner and da Costa reacted to the story of the crash on the hillside road.

If they swallowed it, if they wrote

him off, there was no reason why they should alter anything they had planned.

The cigarette burning almost forgotten between his fingers, Laird deliberately switched his thoughts back to the day he'd arrived in Porto Esco, then tried to recall everything that had happened since, in exact sequence. Something was nagging at his mind, something which might matter a lot if only he could recapture it.

His head began to ache again. Stubbing out the cigarette, he sighed. One thing was certain. Even a slave driver like Harry Novak, working his salvage team flat out, would need at least two full days of preparation before his tugs could make their first attempt to haul the stranded tanker clear.

Till then, the cork was in the bottle as far as the submarine was concerned.

Giving up, he went over and searched Ramos's locker. He found some aspirin tablets and swallowed a couple, then, as he put the bottle back, he saw some cleaning rags lying at the foot.

He grinned, took them over to the chair, picked up Captain Amos's old Smith and Wesson .38, and unloaded the six cartridges from its cylinder. Then, slowly, carefully, he began the job of cleaning the rusty weapon.

As occupational therapy it didn't beat basket weaving. But it had one advantage. If there was a next time and he had to use the gun, he'd feel at least a shade safer when it came to pulling the trigger.

* * *

The time dragged past. Now and again he heard a car stop outside the police station or a low murmur of voices came from the office area. Then, soon after one car had come and gone, Sergeant Ramos came along the corridor and into the room.

"Trabalha," he said grimly. "It is working, Senhor Laird. I have just had Charles Bonner in the office, saying he

had heard you were killed in a crash. He wanted to know if it was true and what had happened." He paused and shrugged. "Senhor Bonner asked a lot of questions — and I gave him answers."

"Think he believed you?" asked Laird, putting down the dismantled revolver.

Sergeant Ramos gave a slow, satisfied nod. "*Sim*. And I told him we haven't identified the two men who were with you in the car, that their bodies were badly burned and we think perhaps they were hitchhikers." Helping himself to one of the cigarettes in Laird's packet, he stowed it away in his tunic pocket. "That made sense, I thought. By now they must know that Miguel and Pedro are missing, with luck they'll think it really was an accident."

"You're getting good at this," said Laird.

"Perhaps it is the company I keep," said Ramos. Then he smiled. "One of my constables spotted that your cell

226

had been used. I told him one of our more prominent citizens was too drunk to go home last night, but that I let him out this morning. It — ah — happens now and again."

He went out, came back with a small bottle of gun oil, placed it silently on the locker top, then left Laird on his own again.

Another hour passed. Laird finished doing what he could to the Smith and Wesson, reassembled it, and was prowling the room in a mood of growing frustration when he heard footsteps again. Then the door swung open and Kati came in, Ramos just behind her carrying Laird's travel bag. Kati looked pale and tired, she wore no makeup, and she was dressed in an old pair of blue jeans and a dark blue sweater. Relief showed on her face as she saw him.

"I've been worrying about you," she said quietly. "I couldn't get along any earlier."

"You're here now." Laird kissed her

gently on the lips, then held her for a moment while Sergeant Ramos carefully studied the floor. "I'm still sorry I got you into all of this."

"I got myself into it." She went over to the window and stood there, looking out through the blind, the sunlight coming in through the slats to pattern across her face.

Behind them, Ramos cleared his throat self-consciously, then eased out of the room, closing the door as he left. For a long moment, Kati stayed silent.

"It's still like a nightmare," she said suddenly, turning to face Laird. "Andrew, I" — her voice held steady and no more — "I killed a man out there last night."

"And I made it two," said Laird softly. "Feel sick about it if you want, Kati. But stop it there. We hadn't any choice — you know that." He led her over to the chair and made her sit down. "Were there any problems at the Pico?"

"None." She brushed back a strand of her long hair, then drew a deep breath. "Nobody knows I borrowed Mama Isabel's car and the pistol is back in her desk."

"How about this morning?"

"Once people heard you were dead?" She winced at the memory. "Mama Isabel was upset, Mary Amos almost cried — then the worst part was the way they both tried to be kind to me about it." She looked up at him. "I played along with it — and hated myself."

"Was José there?"

"He turned up just after Sergeant Ramos left and made suitable noises of regret. He was so — so damned plausible." The words came bitterly. "Then, when I had your bag packed, he offered to run me over here. But I got out of that and borrowed Mama Isabel's car."

"You can call it finished now." Laird laid a hand on her shoulder. "You've done enough."

"No." She looked up determinedly. "I'm in it and as long as I can help I'm staying in it."

Laird didn't argue. "What else has been happening out there?"

Kati frowned. "Well, the salvage tugs have arrived. All three of them were off Cabo Esco at first light and people who have seen them say they're powerful-looking brutes."

"They have to be," said Laird. *Scomber* and *Beroe* and the *Santo Andre* — Harry Novak's little flotilla had arrived exactly on schedule. "Where's Novak now?"

"Out with the salvage tugs. He left the Pico with his two divers straight after breakfast."

"Did I rate a last sad tribute before he went?" asked Laird.

"Not that I heard." For the first time, the beginnings of a smile showed on her lips. "But he wasn't being talkative. Not after the way his evening with Mary Amos ended."

Laird raised a quizzical eyebrow.

He'd forgotten about that little mystery.

"Mama Isabel saw it happen." The twinkle came back into Kati's eyes. "They'd moved through to the bar and he was at the heavy breathing stage. Suddenly Mary Amos just smiled at him, picked up a jug of water, and emptied it over his head. Then she walked out, leaving him like a half-drowned rat."

"One cooled-off captain." Laird chuckled at Mary Amos's revenge, then shrugged. "Harry Novak's one person I'm not sure about — but I think the odds are he knows nothing more than that he has a ship to refloat."

Kati shrugged. "I suppose so." Then she gave a sigh. "Well, what happens now?"

"I wait." Laird saw her expression. "All right, I mean we wait. There's nothing else we can do until this government squad from Lisbon arrives." He paused, then added for emphasis, "I mean it. I stay dead, you stay quiet. Agreed?"

Kati nodded, then glanced at her watch. "I'll get back to the Pico before Mama Isabel wonders what's taking me so long. She reckons we're going to have a busy afternoon."

"Any special reason?" asked Laird.

"Jorges Soller's funeral is at three o'clock. A lot of people will be there — and in the bar before and after it."

Laird said nothing. Dead men didn't usually show up at funerals. At least, not among the mourners.

* * *

Kati wasn't long gone when Laird heard another car draw up outside the police station. Once again voices rumbled in the main office but this time they resulted in Sergeant Ramos hurrying along the corridor. He stuck his head round the door and beckoned urgently.

"*Por favor*, come through, Senhor Laird," said Ramos, who looked flustered. "They have arrived — the people you expected from Lisbon, two naval officers." Then, as Laird followed him back along the corridor, he added quickly, "No one else will see you. One of my men is posted outside."

Two strangers in civilian clothes were waiting in the sergeant's office. The nearest, tall and dark-haired with a thin, raw-boned face, gave a faint but friendly smile of greeting.

"Glad to meet you, Mr. Laird," he said in an unmistakeable New England accent. "Sorry we couldn't get here sooner, but we haven't been loafing around. Formalities first — I'd want that in your shoes."

Laird checked the identity cards the two men offered. The New England accent belonged to Captain David Alder, U.S. Navy. His companion, Captain Filipe Ribeiro, a stocky individual with a mild, almost ascetic face and cool, calculating eyes, was from Portuguese Naval Intelligence.

"We're both attached to the office of the C. in C. NATO, Eastern Atlantic," said Alder. "Our boss wanted to send someone British but you people have one hell of a gift for being on leave when something nasty turns up." He pointed to Ribeiro. "And I'd better warn you, friend Filipe is a lot meaner than he looks. When he goes swimming, you can see his dorsal fin."

Ribeiro grunted, then glanced at Sergeant Ramos, who was hovering discreetly.

"*Sim*, you can stay, Sergeant," he said in a soft voice which held an underlay of unmistakeable authority. "But anything you hear must not be repeated. You understand?"

Ramos nodded and quietly moved a couple of extra chairs towards his desk. Then, while Laird and the two NATO officers sat down, he stayed on his feet in a corner of the room.

"So, let's get started," said Alder, the easy-going humour wiped from his voice. "Laird, you've got hold of something that is going to be damned difficult to handle."

"Particularly from my country's viewpoint," said Ribeiro. "We want to hear all you know, Senhor Laird — from the beginning, and if we question you like an inquisition, *desculpe-me* . . . my apologies."

Alder produced a small tape recorder from a brief case, set it going, then nodded. Laird talked, with the feeling he was telling a story that was getting worn at the edges. But then the cross-examination began, Alder and Ribeiro in turn, each of them probing, questioning, sometimes challenging in detail, totally relentless when Laird hesitated. Even Sergeant Ramos was occasionally dragged in when some local aspect had them puzzled.

At last the two NATO men exchanged a glance and a nod, then Alder stopped the tape recorder. Feeling mentally drained, Laird took the cigarette Ribeiro offered and accepted a light.

"Well, now we know," said Alder softly. "Your submarine sounds like a Russian 'Ula' class — one of their smaller, older boats, conventional diesel-electric propulsion. Yes, it's what we expected. Right, Filipe?"

Ribeiro nodded.

"You knew it was there?" Laird stared at them.

"No." Alder shook his head slowly. "Not till your message got through. But we were certain something was happening somewhere along this coast — for the past week our signals people have been monitoring some unusual high-speed coded radio traffic without being able to get a positive bearing on source." He shrugged. "Plus a lot of other activity. There's a Russian spy trawler loafing just outside Portuguese territorial waters and at least one submarine prowling further out. Air reconnaissance has been keeping tabs on a submarine mother ship with destroyer escort which has quit their Mediterranean fleet and is just cruising around this side of Gibraltar."

"We knew the questions, Senhor Laird," said Ribeiro, and spread his hands. "But you gave us the answers, and we had no idea that arms were being loaded."

"It's brand new," admitted Alder. He built a steeple with his finger tips, frowning. "I mean right here, and now. Hell, it happens in plenty of countries — one man's terrorists are another man's freedom fighters and it depends which side you're backing who does the supplying." He paused and grimaced. "That's my personal, cynical, off-the-record view. But why here?"

"My people are working on a possibility," said Ribeiro. "It is important to us, yet puzzling. This country is still getting used to the idea of being a democracy again and we have our own tensions. Yet — " He stopped there, shaking his head.

Stoney-faced and unblinking, Sergeant Ramos stayed silent in the background. But Laird stirred impatiently.

"What are you going to do?" he demanded. "Just talk about it?"

"Wait for orders," said Alder. "This one goes straight to the top brass — and they'll try to pass it on."

"Senhor Laird, the situation is one of extreme difficulty," said Ribeiro. He saw the smouldering disbelief in Laird's expression and shrugged. "Difficulty and embarrassment — for us as much as the Russians. No wonder they are prepared to go to such lengths to move your tanker."

"Embarrassment?" Laird fought to hold his voice level. "Is that all you call it? What about the way Jorges Soller was killed, and what about last night?"

"Slow down." Alder's face flushed and he abandoned his steeple-building. "Hell, man, use your head. I'm not talking about da Costa or Bonner or their gun-running operation — we can smash that setup once we know a little more about it. But what kind of diplomatic hassle do we stir up if we land ourselves a Russian sub and its crew?"

"Maybe Senhor Laird would like us to go in dropping depth charges," said Ribeiro.

"If she's a Ula class, she's carrying thirty men," said Alder wearily. "The way you tell it, she's surfacing at night to recharge her batteries so it isn't just hull damage — the snorkel system is knocked out. I'd hate like hell to be in her commander's shoes."

"Even with milk and fresh food deliveries," murmured Ribeiro.

"Well, they've got the best salvage man in the business working for them at the *Craig Michael*," said Laird bitterly. He saw the sarcasm was wasted and shrugged. "What about Bonner and da Costa?"

"That's different," said Alder hastily, sounding relieved. He turned to his companion. "Filipe — "

"*Sim*, we know a little about them," said Ribeiro, sitting back and clearing his throat. "It goes back to Angola, about the time of independence. All kinds of strange things were happening, but our files show that there was a strong suspicion that Charles Bonner was something more than just a construction engineer — that he might be giving help to the Marxist wing of the independence movement. It seems there was also doubt about his friend da Costa, but" — he paused and shrugged — "as you know, he came from a good background."

"The son of an army officer who'd been killed out there?" Laird nodded grimly, thinking of Isabel da Costa and what she had already gone through.

"There was reluctance," admitted Ribeiro. "Then — well, Bonner and da Costa disappeared in the final confusion. When they did turn up, they were with a group of people who had been cut off and who had had a bad time trying to get out."

"So now it looks as if they managed to keep their cover intact and came here to set up a new operation. We reckon Bonner is the dedicated professional, with da Costa in it for the money," said Alder. He sucked his teeth for a moment, looking straight at Laird. "From what you heard, you reckon da Costa is going to make some kind of a run with his *Mama Isabel* tomorrow night?"

Laird nodded.

"Well, you're a civilian — officially, a dead civilian," said Alder slowly. "We can get you out, but it just happens you've got an inside track in all this." He paused and grinned. "And I've a message for you from some character called Morris at Clanmore Alliance. He'd like you to keep an eye on things. Will you stay?"

"Yes," said Laird.

"Good." Alder sucked his teeth again. "You know the salvage game. I'd like your estimate on how things go today at the *Craig Michael*, and anything else you can find out." He thumbed towards Sergeant Ramos. "I've already told the sergeant that for now he keeps working normally — he'll get outside help the moment it is needed."

"What about you two?" asked Laird.

"The sergeant spreads the story that two officials from the British Embassy at Lisbon came to see him. Routine, following the accidental death of a British subject."

Ribeiro nodded. "We will be at Tavira, half an hour's drive from here, Senhor Laird. Could you meet us there, after dusk, at the police station?" His eyes twinkled. "It would be good if you could also bring this girl Kati who has helped you — I would like to meet her."

"That's it, then." Alder glanced at his watch, then at Ribeiro. "We'd better move. I don't keep admirals waiting."

They rose and Sergeant Ramos saw them out. When he returned, he went to the cupboard where he kept his brandy bottle. Filling two glasses, he placed one in front of Laird.

"Sergeant," said Laird wryly. "You're

the only civilised man in town."

They drained their glasses and Ramos solemnly filled them again.

* * *

Two hours later, Andrew Laird pedalled his way through the back streets of Porto Esco aboard an antiquated bicycle in the relaxed certainty that even his best friends would have found it hard to recognise him.

The afternoon sun was warm. It beat down on the close-packed little houses, highlighting the brown earthenware flowerpots at their windows and the bright *ulejos* tiles which were the standard ornamentation round their doorways. Sprawled out on the cobbles, a dog barked at him without bothering to get to its feet. Women gossiping outside a shop ignored him and a cluster of children shouted a few pointed insults as he went past.

Laird grinned. He was wearing old serge trousers, a stained, evil-smelling canvas jacket, and a collarless shirt. A greasy, wide-brimmed hat was rammed down on his head and he had a grubby ex-army haversack slung over his shoulders. It contained the cleaned-up .38 and a pair of binoculars borrowed from the loot found aboard Jorges Soller's boat, but for the rest he looked like a wandering tramp.

Sergeant Ramos had produced the clothes and the bicycle. Then he had sneaked Laird out through the mortuary door at the rear of the police station and had pointed him on his way.

The bicycle squeaking and juddering, Laird pedalled on. The houses ended, the narrow road's character changing as it wound through straggling, stunted olive groves and tiny fields where a few thin goats were searching for pasture. Then that ended too and the road became a track which petered out at a boundary fence with empty scrub and grassland on the other side.

He left the bicycle at the fence, climbed over, and began walking. A few minutes later he was crouching on the sea cliff edge of the Cabo Esco headland, a stiff breeze plucking at his borrowed clothes while he looked down at the bustling activity which now surrounded the long, black bulk of the stranded *Craig Michael*.

Several work boats and the small tug from the Companhia Tecnico yard were busy in the narrow space of channel around her stern. But when he brought out the binoculars he trained them first to the tanker's seaward side and the three big, ocean-going salvage tugs which lay waiting some distance out, anchored in line astern.

Scomber, *Beroe*, and *Santo Andre* — he felt an odd, irrational twinge of nostalgia as he focussed on the *Scomber's* familiar, powerful hull and saw the way the breeze was making her aerial rigging quiver. Despite Novak, it hadn't been all bad times when he'd crewed aboard her.

A few men were visible on the salvage tugs, working around the massive towing winches at their sterns. Checking and double-checking, getting ready for the time when their steel wire hawsers, each as thick as a man's arm, would have their turn.

But that wasn't yet. Cupping his hands against the wind, Laird lit a cigarette, then raised the binoculars again. This time he focussed on the clutter of small craft around the *Craig Michael*'s stern. Some were working as a team with the Companhia Tecnico tug, positioning a series of marker buoys vital to the sheer geometry of the effort ahead. Others were being used by the team of divers from the salvage tugs and Harry Novak himself was aboard a small, fast launch which was darting from place to place.

Laird waited, guessing what was coming as he saw the scuba divers surfacing and being hauled aboard their craft. The seconds ticked past, then a series of minor eruptions blossomed in the water below, leaving a froth of white which vanished in the swell while the divers went down again.

Harry Novak was going flat out to remove any undersea obstacle that threatened his success. Cordtex explosive, waterproof charges like thin coils of rope, had always been one of his favourite tools. An instantaneous detonation fuse with a powerful core, it was almost surgically efficient in the hands of an expert. Coiled round any obstacle, the number of strands used a matter of judgement and experience, it could blast and cut in totally controlled style — old hands on the *Scomber* loved to demonstrate that, party-trick style, by using it to chop steel piping into lengths as clean as any hacksaw job.

He stayed on the cliff top long enough to see another series of charges churn the water. Then, tucking the binoculars into his grubby haversack, he made a thoughtful way back to where he'd left the bicycle and began the return journey. Pedalling along the track, cursing the bumps, he hoped Sergeant Ramos had remembered the one thing he'd asked him to do.

The outskirts of Porto Esco were still quiet but as he neared the centre of the town he became conscious of an increasing number of people around him, all making their way down towards the shore road. Dismounting, pushing the bicycle, Laird joined the drift until it brought him on to the shore road and close to the Pousada Pico.

The street ahead was crowded. A little further on, beside the sea wall where his boat was still moored, Jorges Soller's funeral procession was forming up. At the head, his plain wooden coffin rested on a carefully polished handcart. A group of fishermen in their Sunday best stood ready to take the shafts for the walk to the churchyard and other mourners were gathering behind them, men at the head of the procession and women in an equally formal grouping at the rear.

Pushing the bicycle, grunting an occasional apology, Laird moved into the outskirts of the crowd, then stopped again, head bowed, watching the mourners from under the edge of his greasy hat brim. His guess had been right. José da Costa and his mother were both there, and he identified several other faces from the Pico staff.

A stir ran through the crowd as the fishermen took position at the handcart and it started to move off. Then, as the procession firmed and began following, Laird waited just long enough to see that both da Costas were staying with it. Turning away, he went up the nearest side street and from there reached the alleyway at the rear of the Pico.

Kati Gunn stepped into sight as he arrived, stared incredulously at his clothes, then beckoned him in. He followed her, then propped the bicycle against a wall.

"Well, you made it," she said with a note of relief. "In that outfit, I'm not surprised. Sergeant Ramos said — "

"I wanted to talk to you," said Laird.

"That was for his benefit. Kati, I want to take a look around José's room." He saw the surprise in her eyes. "If he's cynical enough to stay with the funeral, it's as good a chance as any."

She hesitated, then nodded. "Everybody but me is out there — I'm supposed to be still recovering from hearing about you being killed. We can do it."

Going down the alleyway, they crossed the Pico's courtyard and through into the empty lobby. Kati went behind the reception desk and brought out a key.

"It's our spare master key," she explained. "José has the first room on the top floor rear and we can — "

"No, not 'we' this time." Gently, he took the key from her. "I've another job for you. Has he a phone up there, one that goes through the office switchboard?"

Kati nodded, puzzled.

"Then stay by the switchboard and act sentry for me. Give his extension two short rings if there's any problem."

The haversack still over his shoulder,

he left before she could argue, climbed the stairs to the top floor, and unlocked José da Costa's door. Slipping into the room, he locked the door behind him again, then looked around.

It was a bigger room than the one Laird had occupied but otherwise much the same, except that José da Costa's personal taste ran to a leather couch, purple drapes, and a king-sized mirror on one wall.

Swiftly, but carefully, Laird set to work searching the room. Apart from a look at da Costa's wardrobe of clothes and the usual accumulation of personal items, his only find was a partly used carton of .22 rifle ammunition. Shrugging, still uncertain what he was looking for, Laird moved into the small washroom area.

The cupboard above the washbasin also yielded nothing. He was turning away when the washbasin itself caught his eye and, on a sudden hunch, he stooped and felt into the space behind it. His fingers moved along pipes and connections, then suddenly brushed something soft, cold, and yielding. Gripping an end, he eased out a package wrapped in oilskin, opened it, and examined the contents with a grim satisfaction.

If nothing else, he'd found José da Costa's survival kit — a small, fully loaded Browning automatic pistol, a Portuguese passport made out to Luis Camacha, wine merchant, and a slim, high denomination wad of U.S. dollar bills.

Three thousand dollars. He set the money aside, examined the fake passport more carefully, and raised an eyebrow at the entry stamps on the visa pages. Da Costa appeared to have used it at least half a dozen times on visits to Spain.

Wrapping the bundle as he'd found it, Laird stooped to return the oilskin package — and at the same moment the telephone in the room gave two short rings.

Cursing, he rammed the package in

its hiding place and headed for the door. He had it opened, was outside in the corridor, and was locking the door again with the passkey when he heard da Costa's voice coming from the stairway, then a rumbled, clipped reply which was unmistakeably Bonner.

He was cut off from escape and every second the voices were coming nearer. Swiftly, Laird tried the next door along the corridor. The handle turned, he opened the door, stepped in, closed it quickly behind him — and found a startled Mary Amos staring at him from the middle of the room. Then, as she saw his face, her eyes widened in horrified disbelief and her mouth opened.

"No," he hissed urgently, grabbing the woman and clasping his other hand tightly across her mouth before she could struggle. "It's all right — but stay quiet. For your husband's sake, Mrs. Amos — just stay quiet."

She still stared at him but managed a nod. Taking no chances, Laird kept his hand over her mouth while he listened to da Costa and Bonner's muffled voices outside and the sound of da Costa's room door open and close. Then, as the voices ended, he gave a sigh of relief and released the woman.

"Sorry," he said softly.

"You" — she swallowed hard but had sense enough to keep her voice low — "you're supposed to be — "

"I'm not." He gave her a reassuring grin. "But right now it's useful if it stays that way."

"Am I supposed to understand?" The colour had begun to return to her freckled face. Sitting down on the edge of the bed, she drew a deep breath. "Does Kati know?"

He nodded, then signalled her to stay silent. Da Costa's room door had opened again. He heard the two men come out and the door slam shut again. Gradually, their voices receded in the direction of the stairs. As they faded, he relaxed and for the first time noticed the small suitcase lying closed on the bed beside Mary Amos.

"You're going back to the tanker?" he asked.

"Yes. There's a boat waiting for me. I should have gone earlier, but I went shopping and then — "

"Then this," he finished for her, thinking fast. "Look, I can't explain yet and I'm not going to try. When you get out to the *Craig Michael* tell your husband I want to talk to him and that I'll get aboard somehow tonight, after dark — probably late on."

"Andy Dawson and the others will have to know." She flushed to the roots of her red hair. "You can trust them."

Laird groaned inwardly, but nodded. "There's one other problem, how I get out of here."

"Is Kati downstairs?" she asked.

"Yes."

"Men." She gave a mock grimace. "Always complicating things."

She lifted the bedside phone before

he could argue, waited for an answer, then smiled and spoke in a low murmur for a moment. Then she hung up.

"They've gone," she said calmly. "Kati says José met Bonner and dropped out of the procession. They came back because he wanted to collect his sunglasses — and it's clear downstairs if we leave now." She stopped him as he took a step towards the door. "Mr. Laird, would you mind carrying my case?"

Ten minutes later he dismounted from his borrowed bicycle at the rear of the police station, tapped on the mortuary door, and Sergeant Ramos let him in.

"Did it go well?" asked Ramos, once he had Laird back in his room.

"Let's say I stayed lucky," answered Laird, stripping off his borrowed clothes and getting back into his own. "Sergeant, let me tell you one thing. Never underestimate a woman — any age or shape. I keep doing it and keep finding out again."

Ramos gave him a puzzled frown. "*Por favor*, Senhor Laird, I don't understand." He paused, the frown deepening. "*Sim*, and I don't think I want to."

Kati came for him in Mama Isabel's Volkswagen soon after dusk and once again he left by the rear door. They talked most of the half hour drive to Tavira, but by common, unspoken consent only a little of it was about what was happening at Porto Esco.

Tavira was west along the coast, at the end of a long inland curve of road, a larger town than Porto Esco, big enough to have a string of tourist hotels and high-rise apartment blocks, traffic lights, and night club bars. They found the police station, parked the Volkswagen in the yard, and went in.

Laird's name was enough. A plain-clothes sergeant took them straight along a corridor to an office where Captain Alder and Captain Ribeiro were waiting, then backed out quickly.

For the first minute or so, the two

men more or less ignored Laird once they'd been introduced to Kati. Alder brought her a chair and Ribeiro fussed around as she sat down.

"In a job like ours, senhorita, pleasant moments like this are few and far between," declared Ribeiro, his mild face beaming.

"What he means is Laird didn't tell us everything about you," grinned Alder, looking her up and down. Kati was wearing a plain blue pants suit with a pastel blue sweater, her tawny hair brushed loose and glinting under the light, and Alder's admiration was genuine. "Thanks for coming. Uh — that goes for you too, Laird."

Ribeiro produced another chair for Laird, then, as they settled, the atmosphere became businesslike again.

"How much does Senhorita Gunn know?" asked Ribeiro pointedly.

Laird shrugged. "Just about as much as I do. She earned it."

"I've no quarrel with that," said Alder, his flat New England voice softening for a moment. "Right, we'd better bring you up to date on a couple of things. First, we're getting the local police to say that the two bodies found with yours in the car have been identified as your pals Miguel and Pedro — Sergeant Ramos is taking care of it. We couldn't let that drift indefinitely. Second, and a lot more important, Filipe's people in Naval Intelligence have come up with a notion where those arms shipments are going."

"Spain," said Laird quietly.

Alder swore pungently, then grunted an apology in Kati's direction.

"Por qué?" demanded Ribeiro. "What makes you say that?"

"A passport — and a hunch." Laird told them how he'd found José da Costa's getaway kit, then went on. "It fits. If he simply wants to meet a contact, he can go in clean, by land. But if he's running a cargo, the *Mama Isabel* could make a round trip from Porto Esco to just about anywhere around the top end of the Gulf of Cádiz late at night and be back before dawn."

"That's how we figured it," said Alder slowly. "That, and some facts. Spain is a future candidate for the NATO alliance now her politics are easing, so contact is better than it used to be. The word is they know there's a trickle of Soviet small arms weaponry being fed to people who'll be happy to use them."

"So why not do it direct?" demanded Laird. "Why a middleman?"

"Think about it." Alder glanced almost apologetically at Ribeiro, who shrugged. "There's a lot less risk in having a base this side of the frontier — they've plenty of friends around, open supporters and the other kind. Then if a Portuguese boat is caught gun-running by the Spanish that's almost an incidental, politically — compared with the alternative."

"He also means our security is weak at the edges," said Ribeiro bluntly.

"But the rest of it, the Spanish interest, is an old tactic. A few armed guerillas pop up here and there. The Left is blamed, the Right react — civil instability is the name of that particular game, Senhor Laird. It can pay big dividends, for a very small investment."

"So when do you do something about it?" asked Laird. "Or are your bosses still playing musical chairs to see who gets left with that decision?"

Alder and Ribeiro exchanged an odd glance, then Alder shrugged and turned to Kati.

"How do you think people like your aunt would like to see this finish?" he asked. "Clean or nasty?"

"Clean." Her mouth tightened. "But it can't happen that way, can it?"

"Not completely, but there are plenty of reasons why we'll do all we can." He swung his attention to Laird. "What's the progress on getting the tanker refloated?"

Laird frowned, reluctant to be too positive. "It's going well — or it seems that way. But I'll know better once I get aboard tonight and talk to Captain Amos."

Once again Alder and Ribeiro exchanged the same odd glance and this time the merest hint of a smile.

"We might help you there, Senhor Laird," said Ribeiro cautiously. "And afterwards — yes, perhaps you could help us with something. That is" — he paused apologetically and glanced at Kati — "if Senhorita Gunn will drive back alone to Porto Esco."

"Why should I?" asked Kati, surprised.

"Because we want everything else to look normal," said Alder. "Just for a little while longer. And we also want someone who can stay close to the centre of things and keep her eyes open. Will you?"

She looked at Laird and he gave a reluctant nod.

"Then I'd better go now," she said crisply, and the others got to their feet as she rose. "The sooner I'm back, the happier Mama Isabel will be. But" — she glanced at Alder again — "you said you'd try to make it as clean as possible, Captain."

"That includes your aunt," nodded Alder. "Laird, stay with me. Filipe — "

Nodding, Ribeiro went with her to the door. She stopped there, looked back at Laird for a moment, then they went out.

"Well?" asked Laird suspiciously as the door closed. "What's the little 'something' you want out of me?"

Alder smiled and spread his hands in a totally un-North American way.

"Hell, nothing much," he said soothingly. "We just thought we'd go and have a look at your submarine."

7

NINETY minutes later a two-vehicle convoy drove away from the police station at Tavira. The Volvo station wagon in the lead carried Laird and the two NATO men. The small, unmarked truck close to their tail had a Portuguese marine corporal in civilian clothes at the wheel and two other marines rode under the canvas hood, which also sheltered a rubber Gemini boat with a small out—board engine.

Captain Alder had elected to drive the Volvo. Keeping to a modest speed, checking his rearview mirror now and again to make sure the truck remained with them, he kept up a placid, off-key whistling as he steered along the road to Porto Esco.

"I forgot to tell you," he said suddenly, breaking off in mid-tune.

"We eased one or two men into Porto Esco this evening — your Sergeant Ramos knows about them by now."

Laird showed his surprise. "Exactly what are they supposed to be doing?"

"*Nada* . . . nothing, or very little," said Ribeiro, leaning over from the rear seat. "Their orders are to wait and watch, Senhor Laird."

"Call it balancing the odds," interjected Alder. "From what you saw, we can calculate on da Costa and Bonner still having half a dozen men, maybe more on their team — "

"Discounting the submarine crew?" asked Laird.

"Hopefully, yes." Alder paused and cursed as an approaching car dazzled them mercilessly with its head lamps, then went on. "So like I said, we're balancing the odds. The boys we've moved in are Filipe's men, hand-picked. The same goes for the three in the truck."

The two vehicles drove on through the night, the sky overhead dark and heavy with cloud. Then, a few kilometres before Porto Esco, Alder slowed and swung off the main road. The truck following, Ribeiro navigating with the aid of a map and a torchlight, they jolted and lurched along a small maze of farm tracks until, suddenly, they saw the sea just ahead of them.

Switching out the Volvo's lights, the truck following his example, Alder coasted to a halt close to the edge of a shingle beach. Switching off the engine, he glanced at Laird.

"From here, we think," he said quietly. "What do you reckon?"

Laird took his bearings from the distant curve of lights which marked Porto Esco on the far side of the bay. They had come some distance along from the Companhia Tecnico yard, though he could just see the lights of the approach buoys to the yard — and the brighter lights which marked the start of the Cabo Esco channel to the open sea were clearly visible.

"As good as you'll get," he agreed.

"Right — and we'll take you to the tanker first." Alder glanced back at the truck. The three marines were already unloading the rubber boat and preparing to mount the outboard motor on its transom. "Let's move."

They got out of the station wagon. Opening the rear door, Ribeiro brought out three sets of dark, one-piece overalls and tossed one set to Laird.

"For later," he said laconically.

They pulled on the overalls and Alder returned to the Volvo, then came back carrying a small leather case. The three marines, now wearing similar overalls, had dragged the rubber boat down to the water's edge and stood waiting.

"Ready, Senhor Laird?" asked Ribeiro.

Laird nodded. They got aboard, joined by the marine corporal who had a grin on his face and was carrying a machine pistol. At a signal from Ribeiro the other two marines pushed them clear of the shingle, then stood watching from the shore as the little outboard came to life and the boat began to murmur out into the bay.

It wasn't a totally uneventful journey. Twice they had to cut the engine and drift, crouching low, while brightly lit fishing boats went past heading out to sea. But the night darkness was on their side and soon they were heading down the Cabo Esco channel with the bulk of the *Craig Michael* like a massive barrier ahead.

The tanker had her masthead lights burning, supplementing the international 'I am aground' message spelled out by the red lamps which showed at her stern. And briefly, as the rubber boat closed, Laird saw other pinprick lights out beyond the mouth of the channel marking where the three salvage tugs lay at anchor for the night.

Alder had one more surprise for him just before the Gemini came in to bump alongside the *Craig Michael*'s accommodation ladder.

"I'm coming aboard with you," he said suddenly. "Don't worry, I'm not going to upset your Captain Amos. But the way things are, I'd better be the one who does most of the talking."

Laird was still first up the ladder. Halfway up, he glanced back to see Alder close behind him and the Gemini rubbing its hull against the tanker while the two men still aboard her sat relaxed but watchful.

They heard a hoarse challenge as soon as they stepped on deck, then Jody Cruft stepped out from the shadow of a lifeboat davit. The lanky, fair-haired bo'sun had a length of lead piping in one hand and lowered it with a trace of disappointment as he recognised Laird.

"The Old Man's waiting for you," he said, with a suspicious glance at Alder. "Uh — Mr. Laird, all of us thought it pretty good you weren't dead."

"I feel that way too," agreed Laird cheerfully. "Lead on."

Cruft shepherded them through a companionway door, then along to the same cabin Laird had been in before.

269

Captain Amos and Mary Amos were both there, but there was no sign of Andy Dawson or Cheung. Once they'd entered, Amos gave a nod to Jody Cruft, who slipped away again.

"I thought I'd keep this private," said Amos, frowning past Laird at Alder. "I've got Jody and the other two taking watch and lookout on deck, just in case."

Laird nodded, smiled at Mary Amos, then gestured toward Alder.

"I've got myself a keeper," he said. "This is Captain Alder. He's U.S. Navy."

"Well, we won't hold that against him," said Amos. "After what I've heard from Mary, I'm past being surprised."

Mary Amos, wearing old jeans and a shirt, wrinkled her nose at the reminder. "When I came back, I had a little trouble persuading him I was serious." She glanced at her husband. "Still, eventually John decided I wasn't mad."

"Your wife helped a lot, the way I've heard it," said Alder seriously.

"She never could mind her own business," said Amos, his dark, heavy-nosed face softening for a moment with a hint of pleasure. "You'll have a drink while you're here?"

They nodded and Mary Amos turned to a whisky bottle and glasses already lying out. She poured four stiff drinks, added just enough water to dampen them slightly, and kept one for herself while she passed the others round.

"You'll want to know what this is all about," said Alder slowly, sipping his drink. He paused long enough to let Amos nod, then went on. "I could lie to you, Captain. But I won't — I'm just going to ask you to take me on trust when I say I can't tell you yet. Except that getting your ship refloated and the channel fully open again is the thing that matters most to — well, certain people we're up against."

"That much I was beginning to gather," said Amos with a heavy sarcasm. "Go on."

"You'll hear some of it later, Captain," said Alder. "That's a promise. But my side of the fence want to see the *Craig Michael* refloated just as much as they do."

Dark eyes narrowing, Amos stared at him, then frowned at Laird.

"I'm just listening," said Laird.

"Then I'll listen too," said Amos. "But understand this, Mr. Captain Alder, U.S. Navy, I haven't much patience left after these last few days."

"I understand." Alder's lean face flushed slightly. "Captain, I want you to obey your owners' instructions. I want you to co-operate to the limit in getting your ship refloated. Is that so difficult?"

Amos swallowed a mouthful of whisky without replying, then glanced at Mary Amos, who had moved beside him. She gave a bewildered shrug, and they both looked at Laird for some sign of guidance. He gave a fractional nod.

"That's agreed," said Amos resignedly.

"Thank you." Alder gave an audible sigh of relief. "Whatever happens you and your people are in no danger, Captain — provided you do what I've asked."

Amos deliberately switched his attention to Laird.

"My owners radioed this afternoon," he said. "They've a full crew on standby, ready to fly out from London as soon as we've refloated."

"What's Novak's estimate?" asked Laird.

Amos shrugged. "Another two full days' preparation, then he'll make his try on the first high tide — which will be around 4 A.M."

"And give the devil his due, he knows his job," murmured Mary Amos. She shook her head. "What I can't understand is why he says we can't use the *Craig Michael*'s engines to help."

"I've told you," said Amos with a slight impatience. "That's the last thing a salvage man wants in this kind of situation. The kind of strain involved could tear them apart — it's a job for the tugs."

Laird nodded. When Novak made his bid, the tanker's role would come down to that of a carefully prebalanced log. Trimming her water ballast tanks, to put an exactly calculated amount of weight astern, was just one of the tasks involved in that process. A salvage deal came down to a mixture of science, skill, and gambler's luck — often enough with the salvage team on a 'no success, no pay' contract deal.

"Good luck with it," said Alder absently, glancing at his wristwatch. "Captain, we've got to go."

They finished their drinks, said good-bye to Mary Amos, and followed John Amos back out on deck.

"You'll keep in touch?" asked Amos as they reached the accommodation ladder.

"Whenever there's a need," answered Alder obliquely.

Amos stayed on deck, watching, while they climbed down and boarded the waiting rubber boat. Then he vanished, and as the little Gemini moved off, lurching as it met a wave coming in up the channel, Laird gripped Alder angrily by the arm.

"Why all that business about being so keen to get the channel cleared?" he demanded.

Behind them, at the outboard's controls, Ribeiro chuckled. The marine corporal was at the bow, apparently only interested in his machine pistol.

"We know what we're doing," soothed Alder, his face a silhouette against the night. "They're innocent bystanders — I don't want them involved."

Laird shrugged, not believing a word of it.

* * *

From the tanker, the Gemini steered a direct course back into the bay and arrow-straight towards the lights which marked the approach to the Companhia Tecnico yard on the north side. But as they passed between the two floating buoys, their boat's small, low shape a mere ripple in the water under the heavily clouded darkness, Ribeiro suddenly cut the outboard engine.

"Now, *por favor*, Senhor Laird, you will lend us some muscle power," he murmured as the Gemini drifted. Alder had already nudged the marine corporal to life and, like the others, Laird found himself with a short, broad-bladed paddle in his hands. Ribeiro grimaced apologetically. "If your submarine captain is sensible, he will have his listening systems manned and we — ah — don't want to alarm him, do we?"

All four men paddling in a slow, steady rhythm, the boat crept forward again while the Companhia Tecnico buildings gradually firmed in a black, unlit line ahead. Then, guided by Laird, they steered their little craft to the right, angling round from the main slipway and quay, until the moment came when he reckoned the hidden deep water creek had to lie almost dead ahead.

"Now," he said quietly.

They stopped paddling and as the Gemini drifted again Alder glanced at the luminous dial of his wristwatch.

"Coming up for midnight," he said softly. "Well, we're maybe a shade early. But if things follow pattern your submarine should show herself fairly soon."

"Stop calling it my submarine," muttered Laird. "I don't want the damned thing."

Alder grinned, then bent down and opened the leather case they'd brought along. After a moment he produced what appeared to be an unusually bulky pair of binoculars. The other item in the opened case was a 35–millimetre camera with a long, fat lens attachment of a kind Laird didn't recognise.

"Infrared image intensifiers," said Alder quietly for Laird's benefit. "You English — "

"British," corrected Laird wearily.

"British," agreed Alder in the same low voice but with a built-in chuckle. "You developed them for gun sights. About the best thing you've done in a long time, next to bringing back real beer."

They waited, while Alder raised the binoculars to his eyes and scanned the blackness ahead. Once he grunted and seemed to be studying something but at the end he lowered the glasses and handed them to Laird without a word.

A moment later Laird found himself looking into the night as if it didn't exist. In its place, the image intensifier lenses showed him a picture which fell not far short of daylight — daylight with a haze of red fog. Adjusting the focus, he sharpened away most of the haze and the Companhia Tecnico yard appeared before him in fine detail from silent, motionless cranes to deserted sheds and outbuildings.

Then, bringing the glasses round in a slow arc, he swore softly to himself as he saw what had interested Alder. The unmistakeable shape of the *Mama Isabel* lay bobbing at a mooring buoy a stone's throw out from the nearest stretch of quayside. Carefully, he checked the launch's low, fast outline again before he lowered the glasses and handed them back.

"That's da Costa's boat," he said in a murmur. "You said we'd time to spare — how about paying her a visit?"

Alder raised a not totally surprised eyebrow and glanced at Ribeiro, who chewed his lower lip for a moment before giving a reluctant nod.

Once more they picked up the paddles and began using them, but this time with a special care and scowls for any stroke that made a noise above a ripple. Within a couple of minutes the rubber hull nosed in against the launch's side.

Swinging himself aboard, Laird landed catlike on the deck and crouched low. A moment later Ribeiro joined him, moving just as silently and with a surprising agility. Keeping an eye on the menacingly near quayside, they crept together towards the enclosed cockpit, found the door unlocked, opened it, and stepped down into the dark, shadow-filled interior.

Ribeiro produced a tiny flash lamp and the little beam made one swift sweep around, from steering wheel and hand throttles to a small, squat radar screen. Then he snapped it off.

From the cockpit they moved on to check the compact cabin spaces located fore and aft, using the flash lamp sparingly. The forward cabin was the larger and Ribeiro pointed significantly at the long, broad deck hatch overhead. If and when the *Mama Isabel* was on a delivery run, the business of loading and unloading her cargo would pose few problems.

It was still incidental. Laird hauled his companion back to a tiny, windowless cupboard of a chartroom located just between the cabin and the cockpit.

There, at least, they could use the torch in safety with the only sounds around an occasional faint creak from the launch's hull and soft swirl of water in her bilges.

Together, sharing the torch beam, they set to work. José da Costa's slim collection of charts covered the southern coast line of Portugal and stretched from there across the Spanish frontier and down the Gulf of Cádiz. But that meant nothing on its own, and the charts were unmarked. A locker held a flare pistol and a collection of signal flags along with a grubby, rolled-up shirt.

That left the shallow drawer under the small chart table. Laird opened it, shrugged at the sight of a slotted set of navigating instruments, and lifted a dog-eared nautical almanac which lay beside them. Then, as he flicked through the pages, a small slip of white pasteboard fell out. He frowned for a moment at the neat handwriting on the pasteboard, then passed it to Ribeiro.

"Mean anything to you?" he asked, puzzled.

For a moment Ribeiro looked equally puzzled. But suddenly his expression changed to a startled understanding.

"*Sim* . . . of course!" Grabbing a pencil from the drawer, producing a cigarette packet, he began hastily copying the writing. "A methodical man, our Senhor da Costa — you know what this is?"

Laird shook his head.

"Try again." Ribeiro tapped the pasteboard. "Two sets of colours — *branco*, *verde*, *branco*, then *branco encarnado*. Think, and add these figures beneath them."

"White, green, white, then white and red," Laird was still lost.

"Suppose they are lighthouse signals," said Ribeiro patiently. "Suppose the figures are compass bearings."

"He locates these two lights, lines them up with these bearings — " Laird understood at last.

"And he has his rendezvous point

along the Spanish coast, where the *Mama Isabel* hands over her cargo." Ribeiro chewed his lip and nodded. "*Sim*, and if we give this to our coastal survey people, they'll pin point it in five minutes."

It was time to leave. They tucked the pasteboard slip back in its hiding place, closed the drawer, and Ribeiro switched off his torch. Leaving the tiny chartroom, they were at the cockpit door when Laird suddenly grabbed his companion, pulling him down below the level of the glass.

A light was moving on the quayside. A moment later it stabbed across the water and flickered lazily along the *Mama Isabel*'s hull. Then it went out as the man behind it moved on and seconds later they saw it shining again, further along the quay.

They got out quickly, found the Gemini still sheltering under the offshore side of the launch, and tumbled in. "Any luck?" whispered Alder in a hoarse, strained voice. He gave a sigh of relief as Laird nodded. "Then we'll get out of this, before that character with the hand lamp comes back."

The four paddles took the rubber boat away from the *Mama Isabel* and as the distance grew, Laird felt the tension draining out of his body. Then, glancing back, the marine corporal gave a warning grunt.

A light was shining on the quayside again. It blinked a series of flashes, then went out — and Alder swore savagely as the surface of the bay ahead and to the left began to churn and heave.

"She's surfacing," he rasped. "Let's move."

The four paddle blades bit with a new, straining effort as they urged the Gemini on. Arm muscles aching, concentrating on his stroke, Laird felt a swell of disturbed water jolt the rubber hull beneath him and caught a glimpse of the long, black shape which was rising to the surface. He heard pumps throbbing and the sound of hatches opening, then voices, and waited for the first shout which would mean they'd been spotted.

It didn't come. Instead, there was the harsh rasp of the submarine's diesels starting up, a rasp which faded almost instantly to a pulsing, air-gulping growl.

"Keep going," hissed Alder. "But use those paddles like you were stroking silk."

They did, for another minute, then stopped as he signalled and all sank down gasping, staring back at the inlet. Shaded lights were moving around the submarine's conning tower, other lights were visible on the quay, and a small boat with an outboard engine was heading out from there towards the submarine.

Still breathing heavily, Alder grabbed the image intensifier camera and began clicking off frame after frame, muttering to himself. By the time he'd finished, the small boat from the quay had reached the submarine and had moored alongside.

"That's it," said Alder softly, laying down the camera. He picked up his paddle and grinned at them in the night. "Home."

★ ★ ★

Fifteen minutes later, using the outboard for the last short stretch, they brought the little Gemini grating onto the shingle beach where the truck and the station wagon were waiting. Materialising out of the night, the two marines helped drag the rubber boat ashore.

Ribeiro had gone up the beach towards the vehicles. Staying with the other men, Laird suddenly saw him crunching back over the shingle.

"Senhor Laird." Ribeiro stopped beside him, his voice strangely awkward. "You had better come. Sergeant Ramos is here, with some bad news."

"Kati?" Laird stared at him with a chill sense of foreboding.

Ribeiro nodded. "Da Costa has her."

He found Sergeant Ramos beside the

truck, his stolid face grim and rocklike in the night.

"What happened?" asked Laird.

"There was nothing I could do, Senhor Laird." Ramos stirred the shingle awkwardly with his feet. "Believe me, if there had been — "

"Just tell it," said Laird. He was conscious of Alder and Ribeiro joining him, but ignored them.

"Senhora da Costa came to me with the story. Some of it she saw, some of it she heard," said Ramos, and moistened his lips. "First, Kati got back from being with you at Tavira. Then, a little later, José came into the Pico carrying a package — a big one. He left it in his room, and went down to the bar." He paused and shrugged. "It seems Kati got into his room — and that José returned and caught her opening the package."

Alder made a questioning noise but Laird silenced him with a sideways glare.

"Go on," he told Ramos in a chilled

voice he hardly recognised as his own.

"*Sim*, senhor." The bulky policeman frowned uneasily. "Senhora da Costa was on the stairs and heard their voices. She went to José's room, went in, and found José holding a gun on Kati." He avoided Laird's eyes. "The girl was on the floor, as if she'd been thrown there. I think — "

"Don't," said Alder softly. "Stick with what you know."

"*Por favor*, I am trying, Captain." Ramos scowled defensively, but obeyed. "Senhora da Costa tried to take the gun from him, but he pushed her away. He ordered her to do what he told her if she wanted Kati to stay alive." He paused, looked out at the night for a moment, and shrugged. "José said she had to keep her mouth shut, that Kati had found out something which could land him in danger. So Kati would have to disappear for a few days, till that danger was past — then he would let her go."

"And she believed that?" asked Laird incredulously.

"They are mother and son, Senhor Laird," reminded Ramos sadly. "She also loves her niece. So she agreed. If anyone asked about Kati, they were to be told she had returned to Lisbon because she was still distressed about your death."

Ribeiro gave a sympathetic murmur. "What else, Sergeant?"

"He told Senhora da Costa that he was involved in smuggling — that he would go to prison for a long time if things went wrong. Then he told her to go back down to the office and stay there. She did, and a little later José brought the girl downstairs and they left the Pico." Ramos hesitated and gave another shrug. "They didn't come back."

Ribeiro muttered under his breath. Alder said nothing, waiting, his eyes on Laird.

"When did this happen?" asked Laird.

"Nearly three hours ago," said Ramos. "Senhora da Costa waited more than an hour, praying for guidance, not knowing what to do. Then she came to see me as" — he winced — "as someone she could trust. She says that for months she has worried in secret about José, with an instinct that something was wrong."

"What did you tell her?" demanded Alder.

"Nothing." Ramos shook his head slowly and unhappily. "I took her back to the Pico, asked her to pretend to do exactly as José ordered — and promised that I would take care of everything."

"And the package?" asked Laird numbly. "What happened to it?"

Ramos looked down at his feet and looked more miserable than ever.

"I looked when I took her back. It was gone." He moistened his lips. "What she saw earlier seemed like a reel of some kind of plastic rope."

"What colour?" asked Laird urgently.

Ramos blinked at him. "Grey, senhor."

Laird swore pungently, and Ribeiro

and Alder exchanged a puzzled glance.

"Cordtex," said Laird. "He's picked up a load of Cordtex from one of Novak's tugs." Then, as he saw they still didn't understand, he spelled it out. "High explosive in a two-hundred-metre reel — that's what he's got. And Kati."

"Sweet Jesus," said Alder, and made it a groan. "That's all we needed."

★ ★ ★

For Andrew Laird, the next few hours were a frustrated nightmare of doing nothing, of being reduced to the role of barely tolerated spectator.

First, Ramos and Captain Ribeiro vanished in the direction of Porto Esco. Then, as the marines faded away with their truck, Alder insisted on Laird coming with him aboard the Volvo station wagon on a return journey to the police station at Tavira. There, while time crept past, Alder talked almost incessantly on a telephone while a series of strangers, some in uniform, others civilians, came and went. Fed sandwiches and black coffee, Laird could do nothing but wait, think of Kati Gunn, and curse at his inability to do more.

Then, at last, they drove back to Porto Esco again through a dawn which was a thick grey mist, a mist which only thinned and vanished reluctantly as the sun came up. The journey ended in a clearing in a pine grove which lay off a side road a few kilometres north of the fishing town.

The marines and their truck were already there. Alder spoke with them, then came back and settled down to sleep across the front seats of the station wagon. Overcome by weariness, Laird followed his example and dozed off in the rear.

When he woke, the sun was high and warm, insects were buzzing, and an unshaven Alder was standing at the opened car door, shaking his shoulder. "Ribeiro and your *policia* sergeant are back," said Alder flatly. "They're waiting."

"What about Kati?" asked Laird quickly, sitting up.

"Sorry." Alder shook his head.

Laird got out of the Volvo and glanced at his watch. It was after 10 A.M. Then, rubbing a hand across his face to get rid of the last wisps of sleepiness, he followed the American. Sergeant Ramos's police car was parked beside the truck, and he suddenly realised there had been other arrivals while he'd slept. A second truck and two cars were parked on the other side of the little clearing, the dozen or so men around them all wearing civilian clothes.

"Filipe Ribeiro called out a few more of his pet marines," said Alder dryly. "They're the kind who go around hoping for trouble."

Sergeant Ramos and Ribeiro were standing in the open beside the truck's lowered tailboard. Tired-eyed but freshly shaved, each greeted Laird with a quietly formal *"Bom dia"* but there was nothing encouraging about their manner.

"Tell him, Filipe," said Alder.

"We tried, Senhor Laird," said Ribeiro. "I checked with the men I had in Porto Esco, Sergeant Ramos used his own sources." His smooth face crumpled unhappily. *"Desculpe-me* . . . it is as if the girl vanished. Except that we know two places where she wasn't taken, the Companhia Tecnico yard and Bonner's cottage. I had a man watching both and they saw nothing.

"She has to be somewhere," said Laird grimly.

Ribeiro chewed his lip a moment. "Somewhere, yes. But — " He didn't finish it.

"But whether she's dead or alive is something else," said Alder bluntly, finishing it for him. "Lets get that out in the open, Laird."

"Yes." Laird knew the American was right. Drawing a deep breath, he turned to Ramos. "What about you, Sergeant?"

"Bonner went to his office at the yard early this morning. As far as I know, he is still there," said Ramos. "José is at the Pico — he arrived in time for breakfast." He gave a slight, humourless smile. "I looked in as usual and we talked, mostly about the weather."

"You saw Mama Isabel?"

Ramos nodded. "I had a moment alone with her. José has told her again that Kati stays unharmed as long as she says nothing." He made a small, angry gesture. "The man is an animal — yet I had to laugh and joke with him as usual."

For a moment there was silence, broken only by the insects buzzing around them. Across the clearing, one of the marines had been brewing coffee on a small stove. Now the rest of the squad were gathering round it, filling mugs and gossiping.

Laird lit a cigarette with fingers

that felt clumsy. His thoughts were on Kati, picturing her smiling face, remembering what she'd done. Now they didn't even know if she was still alive — and the blame had to be his. He looked at Alder and Ribeiro, sensing their sympathy but well aware that whatever they did they had their own priorities.

"We're still well ahead on points," said Alder, as if reading his mind. "We've got to stay that way — which means we don't charge in, grab da Costa, and start banging his head against a wall." He gave a crooked, encouraging grin. "It's going to take patience, Laird. But I reckon the best chance we have of getting your girl back is to play it slowly and carefully — pretty much the way Ribeiro and I had it planned. As long as Bonner and da Costa think you're dead, as long as they think they've the rest sewn up, we've got the best chance."

Ribeiro nodded. "But a new factor is

that they have this Cordtex explosive. Senhor Laird, have you thought why they want it?"

Laird shook his head.

"Think, then," said Ribeiro unemotionally. "Think in insurance terms, which is your business. If the *Craig Michael* salvage should fail, that Russian submarine and her crew could be left bottled up in the bay, hopelessly trapped." He paused, noting Sergeant Ramos's dawning, horrified disbelief. "*Sim*, Sergeant, why not? If a two-hundred-metre rope of high explosive and a delayed action fuse were draped around that submarine's hull the next time she surfaced, with her crew unaware of it — "

"No survivors and the end to an embarrassment," said Laird hoarsely. "But they couldn't get away with it."

"*Por qué* . . . why not?" Ribeiro's ascetic face stayed calm. "With luck, all that would have to be explained in Porto Esco would be a small underwater explosion. The story could be that it was associated with their shipbreaking yard. For the rest, a sad report to their masters that the submarine had failed to resurface. How many questions would be asked, how many people would feel relieved?"

One of the marines came ambling over with an offer of coffee. Alder thanked the man but waved him away, then produced a folded chart from his pocket, opened it out on the truck's tailboard, then faced Laird again.

"Here's something we do know," he said quietly. "Our Headquarters people matched those lights and bearings you and Ribeiro found on the *Mama Isabel* last night. If da Costa does a delivery run tonight, to the same place, we've got his rendezvous pin-pointed — here."

Laird frowned as Alder stabbed a forefinger at a spot on the chart far down the Gulf of Cádiz. It was further away than he'd expected, not far north of Cádiz itself. Then, suddenly, the thin, elusive tendril of possibility which had been with him before came back again.

"You're sure?" he asked.

"Positive," confirmed Alder. "And it's a good one — mudbanks, shoals, and coastal marshland, only one or two small fishing villages. Any Spanish patrol boats around will stay well out from it."

"It's a long way." Laird kept looking at the chart, calculating. Even for a fast boat like the *Mama Isabel*, it would be a four- or five-hour round trip. "And she'll be gobbling fuel."

"Yes." Alder caught on. "So da Costa will need full tanks and maybe more — most of those high-speed jobs are short-range." He turned to Ramos. "Sergeant, can you find out if the *Mama Isabel* takes on extra *gasolina*?"

"My bet is he won't," said Laird before Ramos could answer. "Da Costa wouldn't risk it. Too many people might remember."

Ramos nodded. "There is only one

refuelling dock in Porto Esco, Captain. As *policia*, we keep an eye on what happens there — "

"So maybe he keeps a stock at the Companhia Tecnico yard," said Alder impatiently.

"I didn't see any." Laird drew a deep breath. "But be could have a fuel dump along the coast." He turned to Ramos. "Sergeant, I told you what happened when Kati took me for a drive to a beach north of here. You knew the place — and Kati said da Costa had taken her there once."

For a moment, Ramos's mouth hung open, then understanding showed on his broad face.

"I thought da Costa just followed us that day," said Laird. "But suppose I was wrong. Suppose he'd gone there to do something else, like check a fuel dump? Could it be there?"

"There are caves, Senhor Laird," said Ramos. "One or two are small but deep, and few people ever go near them."

"Suppose that's how it is" — Laird swung round to face the two NATO men — "suppose they've got Kati there as well?"

"We can check it out." Slowly, carefully, Alder folded away his chart and tucked it away. "Da Costa planned a one-way trip for you, maybe that's what he has in mind for her. Filipe's boys can do it."

"I want to go along," said Laird.

"No." Alder shook his head firmly, then gestured towards the lounging marines. "They're pros at that kind of game, and they're only going looking. If the girl is there, we're going to wait until tonight — and you can do the same. If you're right, she'll be safe enough till then."

There was no room for argument. Reluctantly, Laird nodded.

"Good." Alder relaxed and grinned. "Sergeant Ramos better get back to work in Porto Esco. But I could use your help in another direction."

Afterwards, Laird was never sure whether Captain David Alder had really needed him or if it had just been a way of keeping him occupied.

Ramos left first, then Ribeiro drove off with a carload of the civilian-suited marines. Alder disappeared for a spell to use a radio that had been set up beside the second truck and when he came back, looking happier, he beckoned Laird into the Volvo station wagon.

Half an hour later, they lay side by side on the edge of the Cabo Esco sea cliff looking down at the stranded *Craig Michael* and the work going on around her. The picture was much the same as the previous day with work boats fussing around and divers going down. But the three salvage tugs had moved closer, anchored in a tight, new pattern.

"Mainly, I wanted to get the feel of it in daylight." Alder gave up, rolled over on his side to face Laird, and chewed on a blade of grass he'd pulled. "How does it look to you?"

"They're still on schedule." Laird watched one of the work boats closely through his binoculars for a moment. It was using a sounding line, moving in a slow, deliberate pattern between the *Craig Michael* and the tugs. Harry Novak was making his own, exact map of the sea bed, taking no chances about how much water he'd have under the tanker's hull once she was hauled free. "They'll still need all tomorrow, like Amos told us."

"Then the next high tide." Alder chewed at his blade of grass again. "You still reckon they'll do it?"

Putting down the binoculars, Laird nodded.

"Decisions, decisions." Alder abandoned his grass, peered down at the busy scene below for another full minute, then seemed satisfied. "All right, let's go."

They went back to where they'd left the Volvo and got in, Alder taking the driver's seat. Starting the engine, he let it idle, a faraway, thoughtful expression on his thin, rawboned face.

"I want to make a couple of runs past the Companhia Tecnico yard," he said. "But do me a favour and stay low — I'd hate it if things got embarrassing."

At the end of another hour that was finished. Part of the time they sat with the Volvo hidden off the road but with a view of the shipbreaking yard while Alder carefully questioned Laird on the layout of the buildings. Then he stopped abruptly and glanced at his watch.

"Time's up," he said. "Filipe and his warrior band should be back by now, unless they fouled it up. Let's find out."

For Laird, the few kilometres' drive to the pinewood clearing seemed slow and long. But when they drove in, Ribeiro was there — hurrying over to meet them as they got out of the station wagon and grinning from ear to ear.

"You were right, Senhor Laird," he said, slapping Laird enthusiastically on the back. "We found them — two men, armed and guarding a cave about four hundred metres along from where you went swimming." He turned to Alder. "A truck has been there too, and recently. We found wheel tracks — "

"What about Kati?" demanded Laird impatiently, cutting him short. "Remember her?"

"*Por favor*, I was coming to that." Ribeiro's good humour wasn't dented. "Where the wheel tracks stopped, there were footprints — one set small, a woman's feet. And one of the two men always stays by the cave. So — *sim*, I say she's there."

Feeling a relief that left him unable to speak, Laird moistened his lips and returned Ribeiro's grin.

"Sure you weren't spotted?" asked Alder.

"Sure — and we didn't go in waving flags," retorted Ribeiro with a mock indignation. Then he gave a slight frown. "I left a man out there to keep an eye on things. But it would be hard to surprise them in that cave, and with the girl to use as a hostage — "

"We wait," agreed Alder firmly.

Laird stiffened. "Till when?"

"Till the *Mama Isabel* is coming in, and they're busy," said Alder. "Filipe and his team will move when that happens. Then — " He snapped finger and thumb together. "Like to go along with him?"

"Try and stop me," said Laird.

"*Obrigado*, we did think of that," admitted Ribeiro, and shrugged. "But it would be more trouble than it was worth."

★ ★ ★

Waiting has a tension of its own, maybe the worst tension of all. It was that way for Andrew Laird once the initial discussion and congratulations were over, the time still early afternoon and long hours still stretching ahead till nightfall.

306

He shaved and washed, he ate sandwiches and drank coffee, and for a spell he took a hand in a poker game the marine corporal was running in the shade of one of the trucks. Then, unable to concentrate on the cards, he cashed in his matchstick chips, left, and joined the man still on duty at the radio set under the trees.

Laird smoked a couple of cigarettes with him, interested in the radio equipment. It was a compact medium-range unit, and the operator winked as he thumbed to half-a-dozen small walkie-talkie sets stacked beside it.

About an hour later, Sergeant Ramos came out on a brief visit from Porto Esco. He brought a couple of bottles of brandy and word that José da Costa was back at the Pousada Pico, apparently resting in his room. There was still no sign of Charles Bonner, who seemed to have shut himself up in the Companhia Tecnico yard.

When Ramos left, two of the marines went with him. Each carried one of the walkie-talkie sets. Then time dragged on again, while the insects buzzed and the poker players kept up their dogged game.

Then suddenly, almost surprisingly, it was dusk and the mood around Laird changed. The poker game ended and there was a quiet clinking of metal as the marines changed into battle dress overalls and began checking their weapons.

Alder and Ribeiro huddled with the radio operator, listening to the walkie-talkie check calls coming in from the two marines who had gone off with Ramos. One set was located in the mortuary at the police station, the other by some minor miracle was calling from the *Craig Michael*.

"It was Ramos's idea, not mine," said Alder with admiration. "He reckoned he could get a man out there and talk Amos into letting him stay. So now we've got a watchdog on anything going out of the Cabo Esco channel — and I owe that damned sergeant a bottle of whisky. He conned me into betting on it."

Still feeling a spectator, Laird followed Ribeiro as he went over to his men, passing one of the bottles of brandy around, joking with them, taking stock of their equipment.

"What about you?" asked Ribeiro as they reached the end. "Have you a gun, Senhor Laird?" He chuckled as Laird showed him Captain Amos's old .38. "*Bom* . . . at least it will make a lot of noise."

It became dark, with weak, cloud-filtered moonlight casting shadows in the trees around them. Owls hooted out there, a hare died with a scream, and Ribeiro passed the second bottle of brandy around.

Then, exactly at 9 P.M., the radio came to life again. Alder snatched the scribbled message from the operator.

"Ramos, from the *policia* station," he said shortly. "Da Costa is on his way to the Companhia Tecnico yard." Crumpling the paper, he stuffed it in

309

a pocket. "We're in business."

Fifteen minutes later Sergeant Ramos arrived in his car and confirmed da Costa had gone into the yard. For some reason the thick-set policeman was wearing his best uniform but there was nothing theatrical about the dull metal of the machine pistol he was carrying.

Ribeiro signalled and half a dozen of his marines boarded the nearest truck. He nodded, and Laird and Ramos followed them in.

"What about him?" asked Laird from the tailboard, thumbing towards Alder, who was watching.

Ribeiro winked. "He has his own little job to do, Senhor Laird."

The tailboard slammed shut, they heard Ribeiro get into the cab, and the truck began lurching into the night.

★ ★ ★

It was a jolting, uncomfortable journey, punctuated by the grinding change of gears. Inside the truck the marines sat silent, their cigarettes forming glowing pin points of light in the darkness while the air became thick and heavy with smoke.

Laird tried to guess their progress by the way the truck swayed and bounced. But he was still unprepared when they finally stopped and the engine was switched off. Then, after a minute or so, the tailboard was opened.

Climbing down with the others, he looked around at a flat, treeless landscape made neutral by the night. He could hear the sea somewhere close and Ribeiro was standing talking to the man he'd left behind on his earlier trip. Seeing him, Ribeiro dismissed the man with a gesture and came over.

"Any change?" asked Laird.

"*Não.*" Ribeiro shook his head. "They're still at the cave."

"Good," said Laird with some relief. "But where the hell are we?"

"About half a kilometre away," said Ribeiro, glancing past him for

311

a moment, watching the marines unloading their gear. "There's no such thing as a quiet truck engine, so we walk the rest."

They set off soon after that, one of the marines staying to guard the truck. Ribeiro in the lead, they walked in single file for a spell, then he signalled a halt, gathered the little group of armed men around him, and spoke quietly.

One by one the marines melted off into the night until only Laird, Ramos, and the marine corporal were left with Ribeiro. The marine corporal was carrying a radio and another, larger box.

"From here, remember one thing," warned Ribeiro."We are close to them and soon we'll be very close. If they hear us — " He left the rest unsaid.

Ribeiro still guiding, the four men set off again. They topped a slight rise of ground and the white line of the shore was a stone's throw in front and below them, waves creaming in along its length. Keeping low, the others following his example, Ribeiro stopped at the edge of a tumble of giant, broken rocks which led down to the beach.

"Over there," he said in a murmur. "To your right."

It took a moment before Laird's eyes distinguished the black hole which was the entrance to the cave from the other shadows which were being cast by the weak moonlight. Then, as he picked it out, he realised there was nothing easy about their task. The cave was at the base of a sheer face of rock, looking out on a stretch of sandy beach almost devoid of cover but an ideal landing place.

"They'll come out," murmured Ribeiro, as if reading his thoughts. "Be patient, Senhor Laird."

Twenty minutes later a brief glow of light showed at the cave mouth, as if some kind of curtain had been briefly parted. Then a man appeared, relieved himself, paused to light a cigarette, and went back in.

He had hardly gone when the radio at Ribeiro's feet came to life, a low whisper of sound. Taking the handset, Ribeiro answered, listened, then laid it down again with a grin.

"The *Mama Isabel*," he confirmed. "She's on her way — out of the bay, past the tanker, and heading for us."

"The odds are he's running to a schedule." Laird frowned at the luminous dial of his watch. It was almost ten-thirty. "If he is, they'll be getting ready for him."

"*Sim*, and we should be getting ready for them," grunted Sergeant Ramos, reaching for his machine pistol.

Ribeiro nodded, turned, spoke quietly to the corporal, and the man slithered away.

"He'll pass the word," said Ribeiro. "All right, Sergeant, we'll go down. But go carefully."

They inched their way down through the jumble of cold, broken rock, moving slowly, Laird wincing at the occasional faint crunch of gravel underfoot. Then as they reached the start of the sand, Ribeiro swore softly and waved them down.

The same glow had shown briefly at the cave mouth. Again a man came out, walked several paces along the sand this time, and stopped so near to the rocks they could hear him humming to himself. Then he stood waiting, looking out at the sea.

Suddenly, Sergeant Ramos gripped Laird's arm and nodded. A moment later Laird heard the murmur of an engine, then saw a faint line of white wake out on the water and the low black shape of a boat coming in slowly, without lights.

The man on the beach had seen it too. He flashed a torch signal and an immediate reply blinked from the *Mama Isabel*. Turning, still humming, the man went back into the cave.

"Quando?" demanded Ramos hoarsely. "When they come out?"

Ribeiro shaped a snarl at him in the darkness. "When I say, not before. You want the girl, but I want that boat as well."

Tight-lipped, Amos's old .38 in his hand, Laird nodded as Ribeiro's glare switched in his direction. Then they hugged the rocks again as two figures emerged from the cave and walked to a point halfway towards the water's edge.

Much closer but with her engine cut back to give little more than steerage way, the *Mama Isabel* was now clear in every detail under the wan moonlight. She had a man at her bow, standing watchfully with a machine pistol in his hands. But as the torch blinked a fresh greeting from the shore he slung the machine pistol over one shoulder and waved in reply.

Tensely, Laird gauged the distance. Seconds more and the launch should be nudging the sand. Seconds more and . . .

Suddenly, things went wrong. A hoarse shout and a clatter of rock came from somewhere on the far side of the cave mouth, enough to bring the two men on the beach swinging round, guns appearing in their hands. Cursing, Ribeiro jumped up, jammed a whistle between his lips, and blew a shrill blast.

One of the men fired at him, the bullet whining off a rock. Then other shots snapped as Ribeiro's marines raced out of hiding. The man who had fired crumpled and fell. His companion went down on one knee, shooting, and the nearest marine fell thrashing.

Ignoring the shouts and rasping gunfire, Laird sprinted desperately across the sand towards the cave mouth while the *Mama Isabel*'s engines bellowed and her propellers churned a white wrath of water as she started to go astern. The man at her bow was firing, his machine pistol raking the beach at random.

Laird reached the cave mouth, blundered in, tore aside a curtain of sacking, and had a momentary impression of stacked fuel cans and a couple of gleaming battery lanterns.

Then he saw Kati, down on her knees on an old mattress, her hands tied behind her — and she wasn't alone.

Two men, Ribeiro had claimed. But he'd been wrong, just as they'd been wrong in thinking Charles Bonner was snugly back in Porto Esco. Standing over Kati, one hand gripping her tawny hair in a way that forced her head back, Bonner held the heavy Luger in his other hand.

The report was almost deafening in the cave. Splinters gashed Laird's face as the bullet ricochetted off the rock beside him. He fired back, Amos's old .38 bucking in his hand, missed, then hesitated as Bonner started to drag Kati upright as a shield.

But at the same moment, Bonner saw his face, froze in openmouthed disbelief, and Laird fired again. Bonner staggered as the bullet hit him, let Kati go, and the Luger snarled a reply. Pain lanced through Laird's body as the nine-millimetre bullet slammed into his side, low down, sending him half-spinning against the nearest fuel cans.

He heard Kati scream, saw Bonner reaching for her again, and fought back the pain while he pumped the trigger twice more, blindly. The first shot clipped Bonner's shoulder, the second brought only a click as the old revolver jammed — and he saw Bonner's face split in a death's head grin as the Luger steadied on him.

A rasping bellow of gunfire came from the cave mouth, like a giant ripping of steel-mesh calico. Bonner jerked, rose almost on tiptoes in an involuntary spasm of agony, then fell dead, riddled. And Sergeant Ramos charged in, his machine pistol still smoking.

For a moment Laird leaned against the wall of the cave, feeling the blood spurting from the pulsing wound in his side, watching Ramos bring out a knife and cut Kati loose. White-faced in the bright gleam of the battery lanterns, she ran towards him and into his arms.

Then, as he winced, her eyes widened and she stood back.

"You're hurt — " she began, then stopped there as a loud, heavy explosion sounded outside.

They turned, staring out past the torn remnant of sacking.

The shooting had stopped, the *Mama Isabel*'s engines were still going hard astern, taking her away from the shore — but there were flames leaping from her stern.

Swearing, Laird lurched his way out of the cave. A harsh, spitting noise came from above him and an instant later the sea erupted just short of the damaged launch. He looked up, Kati and Ramos beside him, and saw the marine corporal silhouetted on top of the rock face. The corporal raised a small, squat antitank rocket projector to his shoulder again, it spat viciously, and this time the explosion was square on the *Mama Isabel*'s wheelhouse.

But it was only a small explosion compared with the blast which came a moment later, a blast which had an eye-searing core of white fury.

When it died, the launch had vanished.

Laird turned, saw Ribeiro, and staggered towards him.

"Is the girl safe?" asked Ribeiro in a strange voice, his face a pale mask.

"Yes." Laird felt a wave of weakness coming over him as he answered. He grabbed Ribeiro by the arm. "What the hell happened?"

"One of my men was careless." Ribeiro said it flatly. "He slipped — "

"Great," snarled Laird.

"He's dead," said Ribeiro wearily. "The machine pistol on the boat caught him."

"And what about the rest of it?" Laird realised he was shouting, and didn't care. "That rocket projector — you planned to use it, didn't you?"

"If it was needed." Ribeiro nodded slowly.

Laird stared at him, then understood. "You're glad it's this way," he said hoarsely. "You'll say it's cleaner, won't you? You got rid of da Costa, and Bonner's lying dead in the cave."

Ribeiro's eyes widened at the news, then he licked his lips.

"I didn't want anything," he said in the same flat, strange voice. "But ask your Sergeant Ramos which is the best way. Ask him if he'll object to being able to tell one more lie to his Senhora da Costa — that her son's boat accidentally blew up at sea." He licked his lips again. "You wanted it clean, for the girl's sake. It — yes, this way it may not be clean, Senhor Laird. But the problems are fewer."

"And what about Alder?"

"Right now?" Ribeiro shrugged. "He should have taken over the Companhia Tecnico yard."

Laird swallowed, tried to answer, then the night whirled and the beach seemed to come up to hit him on the face.

★ ★ ★

When he came round, much later, he was in a hospital bed in Porto Esco. The first person he saw was Kati, the pain in his side was less, and when he explored, his fingers met a thick strapping of bandage.

Then the procession began. A doctor, who poked and prodded and told him how lucky he'd been, that the wound was clean and should heal without problems. Sergeant Ramos and a pale, dignified Mama Isabel, dressed in mourning black but gripping Ramos's arm in a way that showed she had no intention of letting go. Mary Amos, bringing a message from her husband and the *Craig Michael* crew. And, unbelievably, Harry Novak.

The tug master came in and scowled down at him from the foot of the bed.

"Bastards like you are born fireproof, or the next best thing," said Novak cynically. "I should have known better." Reaching into his pocket, he dragged out a bottle of whisky and dumped it on the bed. "The boys clubbed together for a wreath. Didn't seem worth the trouble sharing out again."

"Novak." Laird stopped him as he turned to go. "Good luck with the *Craig Michael*."

"What the hell has luck got to do with it?" demanded Novak brusquely. "I'm tow master. That's good enough."

Kati came back and he discovered it was already evening. Gradually, feeling stronger, he began to ask questions. She couldn't or wouldn't tell him much and there was an odd evasiveness in her replies.

But none of da Costa's men had survived at the beach, and the marine casualties had been the one man dead and two others wounded. Alder's team had taken the Companhia Tecnico yard and four prisoners in the hired help category, without casualties.

"What about the submarine?" he asked, but a nurse came in before she could answer.

He tried again when the nurse had

gone. Kati shook her head, smiled, and kissed him on the lips.

"Later," she said firmly. "I mean it. You haven't missed much."

He swore indignantly and it didn't help that she laughed.

"Then where the hell are Alder and Ribeiro?" he demanded. "Are they hiding from me?"

"They'll be along." She kissed him again and got to her feet. "You've to get some sleep, Andrew. Then — well, if you behave, the doctors say there's no real reason why they can't let you move over to the Pico again."

Before he could answer, she was gone.

He did sleep because suddenly no one else came and there was nothing else to do. When he woke, a nurse was shaking his shoulder and a slightly dubious doctor was standing behind her.

"Senhor Laird, this is perhaps against my better judgement," said the doctor. "But you can get up and get dressed.

Only, *por favor*, do nothing rash."

The nurse had clean clothes for him, his own, from the bag he'd left at the police station. Then, as he strapped on his wristwatch, he saw the time — and blinked.

It was after 4 A.M. An idea began to stir in his mind, but the nurse was fussing around, trying to get him into a wheel chair.

He waved it aside, stood up, felt his legs almost buckle, grabbed her, hung on, then grinned. She was young and pretty.

"Multo obrigado," he said wryly. "But we're still doing it my way."

She helped him out of the room, along a corridor, and out of a door into the night. Then his grin faded as he saw the waiting ambulance, its rear doors open.

"Don't stop now," said David Alder, stepping out of the shadows. "We've a schedule to meet." The New Englander shook his head. "No questions, not yet."

Obediently, bewildered, he got into the ambulance.

Kati was sitting there, wearing a leather jacket over jeans and a sweater, and Alder climbed in beside them. The door closed, and the ambulance started off.

"Can I ask where the hell we're going?" asked Laird suspiciously.

Alder grinned.

"Then where's Ribeiro?"

"Driving," said Alder.

Kati sat close to him as the ambulance purred along.

Then it began bouncing and rocking and finally it stopped.

"Out," invited Alder, opening the rear doors.

They climbed out into a greying, predawn light. The ambulance had stopped close to the edge of the Cabo Esco headland.

"High tide was an hour ago," said Alder casually as Ribeiro joined them.

Laird looked down and understood. The *Craig Michael* was clear of the channel. Her riding lights burned brightly at her new anchorage well outside the bay and nestling close alongside were the three salvage tugs.

"Clean as a whistle, first time," said Alder with respectful awe. "That damned Novak knows his job." Then he paused and grinned. "But we're right on the button for something else."

A steady, purring engine beat was coming towards them, entering the channel from the bay. Two sets of navigation lights — then Laird stared and swallowed.

First came a small naval launch, flying the Portuguese flag. Then, behind it, travelling on the surface, came the battered shape of the Ula class submarine. Ribeiro went back to the ambulance and flashed its head lamps. Down below, the little group of figures in the conning tower sail appeared to look up. One of them saluted.

Quietly, steadily, the launch and submarine passed through the channel while the first red edge of the sun appeared on the horizon.

"There's a British frigate lying further out," said Alder quietly. "She'll take over as escort till they reach their own kind." He saw Laird's question coming. "It was simple enough. We were on the quayside when she surfaced last night. I talked to her captain, came to an arrangement — then the top brass spoke to his top brass."

"What arrangement?" demanded Laird, shivering a little in the breeze, feeling Kati put a supporting arm around him.

"That we'd let him go and they'd shut down the Spanish operation." Alder's mouth shaped a lopsided grin. "So, officially, it never happened. Except, maybe, if we're forced into it, that a Soviet submarine paid a brief courtesy visit. But if they try anything, we've enough film and evidence to create one hell of a stink."

Laird took a deep breath. "Why?"

"Call it rule number one of the way things are now," said Alder. "When it's real trouble, always leave the other side some kind of option. It works both ways." He paused and frowned. "I nearly forgot. I've a message for you, from some character called Morris who says you sometimes work for him. He wants to know when you'll be fit to travel."

The submarine was still shrinking in size, becoming little more than a hull-down toy now being touched by the first rays of the sun. Laird glanced at Kati and felt her arm tighten slightly.

"Do me a favour," he said. "Tell him I've had a relapse."

They went back to the ambulance.

THE END

A FOOT IN THE GRAVE
Bruce Marshall

About to be imprisoned and tortured in Buenos Aires, John Smith escapes, only to become involved in an aeroplane hijacking.

DEAD TROUBLE
Martin Carroll

Trespassing brought Jennifer Denning more than she bargained for. She was totally unprepared for the violence which was to lie in her path.

HOURS TO KILL
Ursula Curtiss

Margaret went to New Mexico to look after her sick sister's rented house and felt a sharp edge of fear when the absent landlady arrived.

CASE WITH THREE HUSBANDS
Margaret Erskine

Was it a ghost of one of Rose Bonner's late husbands that gave her old Aunt Agatha such a terrible shock and then murdered her in her bed?

THE END OF THE RUNNING
Alan Evans

Lang continued to push the men and children on and on. Behind them were the men who were hunting them down, waiting for the first signs of exhaustion before they pounced.

CARNABY AND THE HIJACKERS
Peter N. Walker

When Commander Pigeon assigns Detective Sergeant Carnaby-King to prevent a raid on a bullion-carrying passenger train, he knows that there are traitors in high positions.

THE MONTMARTRE MURDERS
Richard Grayson

Inspector Gautier of Sûreté investigates the disappearance of artist Théo, the heir to a fortune.

GRIZZLY TRAIL
Gwen Moffat

Miss Pink, alone in the Rockies, helps in a search for missing hikers, solves two cruel murders and has the most terrifying experience of her life when she meets a grizzly bear!

BLINDMAN'S BLUFF
Margaret Carr

Kate Deverill had considered suicide. It was one way out — and preferable to being murdered.

MUD IN HIS EYE
Gerald Hammond

The harbourmaster's body is found mangled beneath Major Smyle's yacht. What is the sinister significance of the illicit oysters?

THE SCAVENGERS
Bill Knox

Among the masses of struggling fish in the *Tecta*'s nets was a larger, darker, ominously motionless form . . . the body of a skin diver.

DEATH IN ARCADY
Stella Phillips

Detective Inspector Matthew Furnival works unofficially with the local police when a brutal murder takes place in a caravan camp.

BEGOTTEN MURDER
Martin Carroll

When Susan Phillips joined her aunt on a voyage of 12,000 miles from her home in Melbourne, she little knew their arrival would germinate the seeds of murder planted long ago.

WHO'S THE TARGET?
Margaret Carr

Three people whom Abby could identify as her parents' murderers wanted her dead, but she decided that maybe Jason could have been the target.

THE LOOSE SCREW
Gerald Hammond

After a motor smash, Beau Pepys and his cousin Jacqueline, her fiancé and dotty mother, suspect that someone had prearranged the death of their friend. But who, and why?

THE DEATH OF ABBE DIDIER
Richard Grayson

Inspector Gautier of the Sûreté investigates three crimes which are strangely connected.

NIGHTMARE TIME
Hugh Pentecost

Have the missing major and his wife met with foul play somewhere in the Beaumont Hotel, or is their disappearance a carefully planned step in an act of treason?

BLOOD WILL OUT
Margaret Carr

Why was the manor house so oddly familiar to Elinor Howard? Who would have guessed that a Sunday School outing could lead to murder?

THE DRACULA MURDERS
Philip Daniels

The Horror Ball was interrupted by a spectral figure who warned the merrymakers they were tampering with the unknown.

THE LADIES
OF LAMBTON GREEN
Liza Shepherd

Why did murdered Robin Colquhoun's picture pose such a threat to the ladies of Lambton Green?

CARNABY
AND THE GAOLBREAKERS
Peter N. Walker

Detective Sergeant James Aloysius Carnaby-King is sent to prison as bait. When he joins in an escape he is thrown headfirst into a vicious murder hunt.

MURDER TO BURN
Laurie Mantell

Sergeants Steven Arrow and Lance Brendon, of the New Zealand police force, come upon a woman's body in the water. When the dead woman is identified they begin to realise that they are investigating a complex fraud.

YOU CAN HELP ME
Maisie Birmingham

Whilst running the Citizens' Advice Bureau, Kate Weatherley is attacked with no apparent motive. Then the body of one of her clients is found in her room.

DAGGERS DRAWN
Margaret Carr

Stacey Manston was the kind of girl who could take most things in her stride, but three murders were something different . . .

STORM CENTRE
Douglas Clark

Detective Chief Superintendent Masters, temporarily lecturing in a police staff college, finds there's more to the job than a few weeks relaxation in a rural setting.

THE MANUSCRIPT MURDERS
Roy Harley Lewis

Antiquarian bookseller Matthew Coll, acquires a rare 16th century manuscript. But when the Dutch professor who had discovered the journal is murdered, Coll begins to doubt its authenticity.

SHARENDEL
Margaret Carr

Ruth didn't want all that money. And she didn't want Aunt Cass to die. But at Sharendel things looked different. She began to wonder if she had a split personality.

LITTLE DROPS OF BLOOD
Bill Knox

It might have been just another unfortunate road accident but a few little drops of blood pointed to murder.

GOSSIP TO THE GRAVE
Jonathan Burke

Jenny Clark invented Simon Sherborne because her daily gossip column was getting dull. Then Simon appeared at a party — in the flesh! And Jenny finds herself involved in murder.

HARRIET FAREWELL
Margaret Erskine

Wealthy Theodore Buckler had planned a magnificent Guy Fawkes Day celebration. He hadn't planned on murder.

TREAD WARILY AT MIDNIGHT
Margaret Carr

If Joanna Morse hadn't been so hasty she wouldn't have been involved in the accident.

TOO BEAUTIFUL TO DIE
Martin Carroll

There was a grave in the churchyard to prove Elizabeth Weston was dead. Alive, she presented a problem. Dead, she could be forgotten. Then, in the eighth year of her death she came back. She was beautiful, but she had to die.

IN COLD PURSUIT
Ursula Curtiss

In Mexico, Mary and her cousin Jenny each encounter strange men, but neither of them realises that one of these men is obsessed with revenge and murder. But which one?